OUTLAW'S PLEDGE

RAY HOGAN

SAGEBRUSH
Large Print Westerns

First published in Great Britain by ISIS Publishing Ltd.
First published in the United States by Signet Books

Published in Large Print 2009 by ISIS Publishing Ltd.,
7 Centremead, Osney Mead, Oxford OX2 0ES
by arrangement with
Golden West Literary Agency

British Library Cataloguing in Publication Data
Hogan, Ray, 1908–
    Outlaw's pledge
    1. Western stories.
    2. Large type books.
    I. Title
    813.5'4–dc22

ISBN 978–0–7531–8264–2 (hb)

Printed and bound in Great Britain by
T. J. International Ltd., Padstow, Cornwall

CHAPTER
ONE

Frank Garnett stood motionless at the edge of the barn's doorway and considered the blackness within the squat, makeshift structure. Hat pulled low on his head to shield his eyes from the driving Kansas sun, his right hand was poised above the pistol on his hip.

Behind him, in the yard of the homesteader whose name he had not troubled to obtain, life went on as usual — two dozen or so clucking chickens scratching in the loose dirt, a cow placidly chewing her cud, several crows scrambling about as they competed for scraps of food, watched by the hogs in their malodorous pen.

But at the sod-and-wood shanty a short distance away, where the squatter and his family lived, there was neither sound nor movement. They waited in the breathless hush for the violence that was sure to come. Even the dog, a lean black-and-tan hound that had greeted Garnett with volleys of furious barking that morning when he rode in, had withdrawn into the shadows beneath the shack.

It had been a long chase for Frank Garnett. He'd picked up the reward poster on Lige Webster in Arkansas's Fort Smith. The dark, bewhiskered face on the dodger had looked familiar, and the cash value placed on the man — guilty of murdering a farmer, his wife, and two daughters in Tennessee — was a nice, round five hundred dollars. Delivering an outlaw he already had in custody to the Fort Smith authorities and collecting the bounty due, he had set out at once to bring in Webster, whom he recalled seeing in a town on the Missouri border.

Arriving there, he'd found that Lige had ridden out — but only the day before — and he'd hurried on; there were not too many five-hundred-dollar rewards being posted, and he was determined not to let Webster get away.

Garnett had caught up with the killer that next morning. From the distant swell he'd watched the outlaw ride into the homesteader's yard and impose on their hospitality. At that point Frank Garnett had closed in, fearing that the squatter and his family could suffer the same fate as Webster's previous victims if he did not act immediately.

Webster, aware of someone on his trail and displaying the cunning that had kept him alive so far in a life of lawlessness, had slipped out of the shack through a window and by way of brush and weeds and various pens had made it to the barn.

Had it not been Frank Garnett that Webster was dealing with, the trick might have worked. But he was up against a man who for years had made his living tracking down and bringing to justice those male-factors whom the regular lawmen felt either it was prudent to ignore or that they simply hadn't the time to

2

spend chasing for weeks or perhaps months. Alert for any change in the scene as he approached, Frank had seen the outlaw come from the far side of the homesteader's shack and, hunched low, leg it for the larger building.

Garnett felt better about the safety of the man and his family when he saw Webster make his move. The killer could have chosen to make his stand in the shack, using the homesteaders as hostages or even shields, but he had ignored that possible advantage, evidently hoping to take the man trailing him by surprise and from a position where he would have a much better range of vision.

Again Webster was guilty of underestimating his pursuer; Garnett, keeping out of sight as much as possible, and after cautioning the homesteader to remain inside his house, had circled wide, and after making certain the barn had no other exit, dismounted and silently made his way to its entrance. Now tense, but cool as winter's wind, Frank Garnett prepared himself to bring the grim hunt to an end.

"Webster!" he called. "I've got you trapped in there — give it up!"

There was a brief silence before the outlaw replied. "Go to hell — whoever you are."

"Name's Garnett. Been tracking you since —"

"I seen you dogging my tracks. You a damned lawman?"

"No. I —"

"A lousy bounty hunter — that's it, ain't it?" Webster said in disgust. "I might've figured."

"I'm giving you a chance," Garnett said coolly. "Can come with me setting in your saddle — or slung across it. Choice is up to you," he added, and ducking low, darted through the doorway into the first stall, occupied at that moment by an aging gray horse.

The outlaw had failed to note Garnett's change of location. "What's up to me is that I ain't letting you take me one way or the other — and I ain't cashing my chips, either!"

Frank listened carefully and pinpointed the outlaw's voice as coming from the rear left corner of the barn. He couldn't see just what was there — probably sacks of feed stored for future use, or possibly bits of lumber brought in out of the weather, or it could be simply an empty stall. The advantages and disadvantages were about even, Garnett realized; Webster faced the glare of daylight outside the barn's entrance, while he had to contend with the darkness of the building's interior.

"Time's about up, Lige," he said, hoping against heavy odds that the man who had mercilessly ended the lives of four persons — after torturing the women — would throw down his gun and surrender. "I'm not aiming to do any jawing or bargaining."

"Then you best figure on coming in after me," Webster shot back. "'Cause I ain't feeling kindly about doing you no favor."

Garnett shrugged in the half dark of the stall and leaned against the gray. Men like Lige Webster never made it easy, and he reckoned that was to be expected. The outlaw faced the gallows for the murder of the farmer and his family, and likely, if the truth could be determined, there were additional instances where murders of a similar nature had been committed.

Garnett glanced about. He needed something with which he could attract the killer's attention, and thus his fire. It would be foolish as well as suicidal to step out into the open and give Lige the first shot. A short length of wood lying in the litter near the manger caught Frank's attention. Apparently it had been used to prop open the feed box in the wooden trough. Retrieving it, Garnett removed the fringed deerskin jacket he was wearing, and inserting the stick through one sleeve, allowed the garment to hang loosely from it. Drawing the bone-handled .45 holstered at his side, he then moved to the end of the stall.

"I'm done talking, Webster. Throw down your gun and come out — hands over your head."

"Ain't a chance!" the outlaw replied. "It's me that's holding all the high cards."

"Maybe. Anyway, it's up to you," Garnett said, and thrust the jacket out into the runway.

Immediately the blast of two quick shots shattered the stillness inside the barn. Garnett, reacting instantly, dropped the jacket and fired straight into the bright orange blossom of the outlaw's weapon.

Webster yelled as Frank jerked back behind the protective wall of the stall and triggered his pistol for a third time. Garnett heard the lead slug thud dully into the thick timbers of the separation, but knew the outlaw had already been hit and was probably down. But he was far too wise to take that for granted. Once before, in a year long past, he had assumed his man was down after a similar encounter and had almost paid with his life for the mistake.

"I'm hit —"

Lige Webster's voice, coming from beyond the drifting smoke, was low and filled with pain. Frank took up the jacket, still hanging from the length of wood, and moved to the front end of the stall again. Webster was probably mortally wounded.

Again extending the jacket into the runway area of the barn, but this time pulling himself erect, Frank peered over the top of the stall. In that instant of time, he saw movement on the dusty floor, saw again the flash of the outlaw's gun. Once more Garnett fired — this time having the silhouetted torso of the killer at which to direct his bullet.

Lige Webster cursed and, on his knees, struggled to draw himself upright in the smoke-filled half dark. For a long breath he hung there, and then suddenly releasing the weapon he was clutching, he toppled to one side.

Garnett leaned back against the trembling old gray and let the tension drain from his taut shape. Then throwing the stick into a corner, he drew on the deerskin jacket, ruefully taking note of the holes left by Webster's bullets as he did, and flipped open the loading gate of his pistol. Rodding out the spent cartridges in the weapon's cylinder, he replaced them from the supply in the loops of the belt that encircled his waist.

Only then did he step into the runway and move slowly toward the prone shape of the outlaw.

CHAPTER
TWO

Both of his bullets had driven into Lige Webster's body, Frank saw when, with pistol still in his hand, he looked down at the outlaw. The first had struck the man in the upper chest, the second almost dead center. Holstering his own weapon and thrusting the outlaw's under his belt, Garnett reached down, took Webster by the arms, and dragged him into the yard.

At once the homesteader, aware now that all danger from the outlaw was gone, rushed into the open, and trailed by his wife and several small children, hurried up. The man — tall, lean, unshaven, and burned red by the sun — stared at the outlaw for a long minute and then shook his head.

"I reckon he was a bad one," he murmured. "Sure did talk plenty mean to me and the missus. You the law?"

Garnett shrugged. "Not the kind that wears a star, but outlaws are my business."

"What'd that fellow done?" the woman wanted to know.

"Murdered a family down in Tennessee. Was what I thought you folks might be in for when I saw him ride into your place."

The woman shuddered. "Sure am powerful glad you showed up."

Frank, conscious of the homesteader's hard, steady gaze, permitted himself a half smile. He knew what was in the man's mind.

"Something bothering you?" he asked.

The homesteader dropped his eyes. "Was what you said. I reckon you're what folks calls a bounty hunter."

"Expect so," Garnett replied coldly and turned to get his horse, tethered at the side of the barn. He paused, then laid his hard glance on the squatter. "That bother you?"

The tall man stirred. "Well, it's just what they say about your kind."

"My kind?"

"Yeh, you know — that you don't give a hoot in hell how you get a man — and that you'd sooner bring him in dead as alive — just so's you can collect the bounty."

"Some truth to it," Garnett said indifferently. "I'm in it for the money, sure, but I leave it up to the man I'm after whether he wants to come in peaceable or go for his gun. It's his choice."

"I sure ain't a'caring how you got him," the woman said, still staring down at Webster. Her children were now gathered around her, looking on, and the family dog, having stirred himself from the shadows, was standing nearby, sniffing suspiciously.

"I'm just mighty glad you come along when you did," she continued. "We was all real scared . . . Now, we're fixing to eat a bite pretty quick. If you'll come up to the house, I'll set a plate for you. We won't have anything fancy, but there'll be plenty of it."

Frank Garnett smiled, touched the brim of his flat-crowned hat. "Obliged, but I'd best be loading up and moving on."

"You live close to here?" the homesteader asked.

"McCurdy —"

The man nodded. "I know the place — was there once a while ago. It's about a day's ride from here. That where you're taking this fellow — whatever his name is?"

"Webster," Garnett said, starting again after his horse. Once more he paused. Reaching into a pocket for several small coins, he handed them to the homesteader's oldest boy. "I'll be obliged if you'll fetch his horse for me while I get mine," he added, and moved on.

A half an hour later Frank Garnett was astride his bay and leading the black Lige Webster had been riding. The outlaw's body, wrapped in the square of canvas Garnett carried for that purpose, was hung across the saddle of the black and lashed securely so there would be no chance of it slipping off. It was a grim arrangement, but a practical one, and Frank had learned long ago not to let it trouble his conscience, for the men he brought in under such circumstances were usually cold-blooded killers, and to his way of thinking, deserved no better.

As he rode steadily westward across the plains and occasional hillocks of Kansas, Garnett thought of how good it would feel to be home again. He'd been away for several months, and while home was nothing more than a small house — a shack by most standards — occupied by him and his brother, Turner, it was the nearest thing to such that they had enjoyed since the family farm in Virginia had fallen victim to the war.

As was the way with so many, the conflict had left them with nothing. In their case, however, the problem was maximized by the fact that Turner had suffered a serious wound shortly before the fighting officially ended in a clash with Union soldiers. The incident had occurred in Kentucky, and Frank, a raw, young volunteer, had been with his brother at the time. Together they had fled before the vengeful platoon of blue-backs across Kentucky, Indiana, Illinois, and into Missouri, where a farmer, taking pity on them, hid them from the soldiers.

Frank had been little more than sixteen, but he had assumed the care and protection of Turner, ten years his senior, with no difficulty. They had remained with the Missouri family for several months after the blue-backs had turned away, during which period Turner made his recovery and Frank paid for their keep by helping to work the farm.

Eventually they moved on, Turner as near to being well as he would ever be, but actually facing a life of semi-invalidism. They drifted first into Indian territory, but finding nothing there by which they could support themselves, moved on into Arkansas. There Turner, always a fair hand with cards, further sharpened his skills to the point of becoming a recognized — and respected — gambler, while Frank, old beyond his years, went from job to job and finally settled down to being a sheriff's deputy.

The work appealed to him, and he was eventually offered a better paying position of like nature in Abilene. He and Turner moved to the booming Kansas cattle town — but their time there was brief. The following year Abilene's councilmen decided they no longer desired the herding business and the hell-raising that went with it and put an end to the settlement's role as a terminus for the cattle drives coming up from Texas, New Mexico, and other ranching centers.

Frank and Turner had moved on at that point, heading for another Kansas town, McCurdy, well to the west and on the Nebraska line. Both men by that time had become experts in their chosen fields, and as McCurdy occupied a strategic location on both the north-south and east-west flow of traffic, they felt their opportunities would be more than ample.

For Turner such proved to be true, but there was no need for a gun-sharp lawman like Frank. A town marshal with volunteer constables at his beck and call, supplemented by periodic visits from the sheriff and his deputy, made the hiring of someone with Frank's qualifications unnecessary.

It was no great problem for Frank Garnett. He had become aware of the large rewards offered by various states and territories for the capture of certain outlaws during his tenure as a deputy in Arkansas, and later in Abilene. Since Turner was now as strong as he would ever be, and thus able to care for himself, turning to bounty hunting was a natural solution for Frank.

It had proved to be a successful decision. In that first year Frank had tracked down and brought in five notorious and badly wanted outlaws, receiving generous rewards for their capture. Turner Garnett, in turn, had established himself as an honest and expert man at cards. He was welcomed in all of the settlement's saloons.

He and Turner had fared well after all, Frank thought that midday as he halted in a small grove to rest and water the horses and partake of the lunch the homesteader's wife had insisted on preparing for him.

True, they had lost everything in Virginia — a good farm, a fine old house with its accompanying outbuildings, which had been in the family for generations — but they had managed to stay alive and carve out a life for thcmsclves in new country.

McCurdy had provided them with a permanent base, a home, and while it consisted of no more than a small piece of ground and a three-room structure, it was theirs, and both had intentions to stay.

With the five-hundred-dollar bounty he'd be getting for Lige Webster, Frank was now entertaining the idea of building onto the house — adding at least two more rooms. For the past year Darla Grace — one of the women in the saloon where Turner spent most of his time — had showed signs of wanting to make her and Turner's occasional stints of living together more permanent. Lack of privacy when he was in town was probably the principal impediment, Frank had realized, and if additional rooms were added, the problem would be solved. It would be fine for Turner; he needed a woman to look after him and supply all the comforts that life had denied him in the past.

As for himself, there was Jenny Pittman — a girl just turned twenty — who was looming more and more important in Frank's life. He felt a warmness pass through him as his thoughts turned to her. She was the daughter of a homesteader and presently served as a waitress in a McCurdy restaurant owned by her aunt. Garnett had hesitated to get serious with her, feeling that he had little to offer in the way of a future. But maybe she would have thoughts of her own on the subject, he had come to conclude, and so he was determined to talk with her when he got to town and see just how she felt about a man who made his living tracking down and bringing in wanted outlaws — quite often dead.

That thought sobered Frank Garnett. Could Jenny, or any woman, ever want to make a life with a man engaged in such a profession?

Stilled, Garnett stared off across the stub-grass-covered flats. Tall, solidly built, with a square-cut face, dark eyes and hair, a full, sweeping mustache and a ragged beard, thanks to necessary neglect, he had the keen look of a hunter.

The red bandanna he wore about his neck was faded, as were the gray shirt and brown cord pants. His once black stovepipe boots were scarred by many passages through stiff and thorny brush, and the fringed deerskin jacket, the worse now for Lige Webster's bullets, hung in straight lines from his wide shoulders, while the plainsman-style hat on his head was tipped sharply forward to turn away the bright sunlight.

For several long minutes he was a rigid, motionless figure as he thought of Jenny Pittman. A strong, fearless man, veteran of a half a hundred violent encounters with desperate and deadly outlaws, he was curiously intimidated by this pert, blue-eyed slip of a girl.

Finally he shrugged, and relegating his consideration of Jenny and her possible reaction to his proposal for their future together to the moment when he would meet her and put his hopes into words, Frank turned to his horse, mounted, and with Lige Webster's black trailing at the end of a lead rope, struck off again for McCurdy. He should reach the settlement near dark, he figured.

CHAPTER
THREE

Smoke was curling up into the hazy, late afternoon sky, marking the time of supper preparation, when Frank rode into McCurdy. Swinging wide of the main street to avoid displaying the black with its grisly burden, he rode in behind the jail and pulled to a stop. Immediately Marshal Amos Carter came forth to meet him.

"Seen you coming," the elderly lawman said in a tight voice. "Wanted to catch you first off, tell you about your brother."

Garnett, in the act of removing his lead rope from Webster's horse, swung around quickly. A frown hardened the corners of his mouth.

"What about Turner?"

"Been arrested — locked up —"

Frank's eyes narrowed. "What for?"

"Ain't sure. The sheriff said —"

"Sheriff? Tom January? He the one who jugged Turner?"

"Yeh, him and that smart-aleck deputy, Cheyenne Jones. Been hanging around town for nigh onto a week. Yesterday they come waltzing in here, big as you please, with your brother all hand-cuffed and such."

"Why?" Frank asked again.

Carter rubbed at his neck in agitation. "Like I said, I ain't got it straight and they won't tell me much. It's got something to do with him being mixed up with a couple other fellows in a holdup. Hell, they just come in and took over my jail like I was nothing. Sure was hoping you'd show up."

"Turner all right?" Garnett asked.

"Just so-so. January sort of rousted him some bringing him in — but ain't bad hurt."

Frank nodded, finished with the lead rope, and paused to give the old marshal's words thought. "January knows Turner's in no shape to put up a fight — not with him or anybody else. Would be no need to get rough. I aim to have a few words with Tom about that."

Carter's attention had finally settled on the canvas — wrapped body draped over the black. "Who you got there?"

"Name's Lige Webster," Garnett replied, handing the outlaw's pistol to the marshal. "There's a reward of five hundred dollars out for him. I'll be obliged to you, Amos, if you'll fix up the papers for me and turn Webster over to the undertaker for burying. You say January's been around for a week?"

Carter reached for the bridle of the black and took a firm grip on it. "Maybe a few days more. He's been on a real gambling spree this time."

"About the only reason he ever comes around," Frank said. "He winning or losing?"

16

"Well, he's bucking your brother like he always does, but from what I hear he ain't been running in luck. Somebody said he's owing Turner about three hundred dollars."

"That's no reason for Tom to lock him up. Got to be something else."

"You think the sheriff could be getting back at you?" Carter suggested. "He ain't exactly an admirer of your'n, specially after you brought in that Mex killer he was out to get. And now your showing up with another owlhoot that's got a big price on his head ain't going to set good atall!"

"Maybe," Garnett conceded. "The sheriff's always figured I was trespassing on his job, but that's how it is most everywhere — even when it's a case where they've backed off from going after some shootist they've pegged as too risky to jump. You're right — he could be taking his grudge against me out on Turner — but I sort of doubt it. Turner's girl — Darla — she all right?"

"Worried a'plenty," the town marshal said. "Been over here two or three times since Turner got locked up. She's scared that him getting knocked around'll stir up some of his old misery."

Garnett's jaw tightened and a hardness came into his eyes. "January's got some explaining to do," he murmured.

On the far side of the jail a man's voice shouted, and there followed the quick beat of a horse breaking into a gallop. The day's heat had decreased, and the pleasant, amber-tinted time that precedes darkness was settling over the town. The smell of woodsmoke and cooking food hung in the motionless air, and from somewhere came the sound of a piano. Frank savored these moments thoughtfully. After a bit he shrugged. His homecoming would have been most enjoyable were it not for the fact that Turner was in trouble. He turned his gaze to Amos Carter once again.

"What about this holdup?" Garnett asked impatiently, anger now showing in his voice. "It happen around here?"

"The sheriff ain't doing no talking about who the other fellows were or who got robbed. He's mighty close-mouthed about it — and he's taking Turner up to the county seat in the morning to stand trial."

"Why the hell there? The judge comes by here once a month."

"Just what I told Tom, but he said for me to keep my nose out of it — and that's what's riling me so all-fired much! This here's my town, dammit! I'm the law — the marshal — and he ain't got the right to come sashaying in here any time he gets the notion and take over! He treats me like I was a swamper or a stablehand."

Garnett was only half listening now. There was something wrong with the whole affair. First off, Turner Garnett would never let himself get mixed up in a holdup. There was no need — he had plenty of money, and if for some reason a time came when he needed more, he knew he had only to ask. They had been that way since childhood, and the war, with its disastrous results, had strengthened the bond between them. What was Frank's was Turner's. Frank also knew that Turner

18

lacked the health to undertake anything as tense and active as a holdup.

There had to be some other reason why Tom January had thrown his brother in jail and planned to hurriedly bring him to trial, Frank realized. And the fact that the lawman intended to have the trial held in a distant town — his own area — made it apparent that all was not as it should be. Garnett was glad he'd returned to McCurdy when he did. Another day or two and he would have found Turner already in the penitentiary, most likely!

"Mind dropping my horse off at the house as you go by? Just leave him in the yard," Frank said. "I'd like to talk to Turner — see if he knows what this is all about."

"Sure thing," Carter said, taking the bay's lines, and then added, "I'm sure glad you showed up, Frank. There's something mighty rotten about this deal, and I just can't seem to do nothing about it. I figure you can."

Garnett nodded grimly. "You can bet I'm going to try," he said, and turned toward the door to the jail.

CHAPTER
FOUR

Entering the lawman's small office, which was not yet touched by the evening's coolness, Frank Garnett crossed to the narrow corridor at the rear, off which were two cells.

"Turner," he called, halting at the first.

His brother, string tie loose, shirt collar open, dark frock coat splotched with dust, rose from the slatted cot upon which he had been slumped and moved stiffly up to the bars. The left leg of his trousers was torn, and his shoes, ordinarily polished to a high gloss, were dull and old looking.

Anger again spread through Frank. "That damn two-bit Tom January — I'm going to take him apart bit by —"

"Forget it," Turner Garnett cut in, grasping two of the bars as if for support. "I ain't hurt none — and there's no sense in you getting yourself crosswise with the law over nothing."

"Nothing!" Frank echoed. "You look like he worked you over good! And you're locked up in a stinking jail — you say that's nothing?"

"Messed me up some, all right," Turner said in his quiet way. Tall, like his brother, he was of a slighter build — small-boned as some would say — and had the same dark hair and eyes. But due to the ravages of his wounds, his face was sharp and sallow. "Got most of this dirt falling down."

Frank studied his brother more closely. He doubted the latter statement; Turner was simply trying to keep him leveled off and prevent him from going out after Sheriff January.

"Maybe," the younger Garnett said. "You going to tell me what this is all about — what you're doing here? Carter said something about a holdup."

Turner shrugged. "That's what the sheriff's claiming. I had nothing to do with it."

"What about the two jaspers that had a hand in it?"

"I know them — Dave Hoskins and Artie Peters. Played cards with them a few times at the Jubilee."

"That all — nothing more?"

Turner Garnett grinned wryly, his pale, gaunt features almost skull-like in the poor light. "You shooting questions at me like that puts me in mind of Pa when he'd catch me in a fix of some kind. Ought to be the other way around — me being older."

Frank smiled. It had been ten years and a bit more since he'd been forced by circumstances to take over and be the head of the Garnett family — such as it was, after Appomattox. Ever since the escape into Missouri and the subsequent departure from farmer Benbow and his lifesaving hospitality, it had been up to the younger brother to care, provide for, and protect the older.

It was a fact never mentioned by either, although Turner showed his appreciation in many ways. That he was now shamed by what had befallen him was apparent in his efforts to minimize the situation.

"What about Hoskins and Peters? Did they pull off a holdup somewhere?" Frank asked.

"So I'm told. Don't know where."

"Then how'd January tie you into it?"

"Can only tell you what I've heard, Frank. Dave and Artie got caught the day after the holdup — robbed some rancher walking around with a lot of money from a cattle sale in his pocket. There was another man with them, but he got away. The sheriff claims they confessed and said I was him."

Frank swore. "Now that's something I can clear up mighty quick! Where are they — Hoskins and Peters? Don't see them in here."

"January's got them in jail over in Johnsburg. They're going to be tried there," Turner replied. Drawing a handkerchief from the inside pocket of his coat, he mopped wearily at his drawn face. "I'm being taken there tomorrow for the same thing — a trial."

Frank Garnett again swore. "It'll blow up in January's face when Hoskins and Peters — and that rancher — get a look at you —"

"They were all wearing masks —"

The younger man was silent as he gave that thought. Somewhere nearby a dog was barking frantically, and the melodic plinking of a piano could still be heard.

"Hard to figure out how they could have named you — if they did," Frank said slowly. "You say all you ever did was play poker with them?"

"About all. Did take them down to Minnie Johnson's house and introduce them to the girls. They asked me to — as a favor. Minnie's been having so much trouble with trailhands that she's had to draw the line, stick to regular customers. I couldn't see any harm in taking them there."

"I don't either," Frank agreed. "Unless maybe January made something out of it. You leave them there, or did you stick around?"

Turner shook his head. "Left them after fixing them up with a couple of Minnie's girls. I was on my way home. Darla had cooked up a good meal for me — and I wasn't feeling so pert. Aimed to take the rest of the night off."

"That the same night this cattleman got held up?"

Turner's thin shoulders stirred. "Not sure of that, but I think it was."

Frank settled back, folding his arms across his chest. He was tired from the long day, but he was thinking little of himself — only of the predicament, a dangerous one, that he had found his brother in.

"The whole thing's got a stink to it," he said. "Tom January's keeping it plenty hushed up, Carter says, and he thinks there's more to it than this holdup business. Can you come up with some other reason why Tom wants you out of the way?"

Turner rubbed at his jaw. "No, sure can't —"

"I know he blows in here every now and then to catch up on his womanizing and gambling. It's the only time he ever comes down into this part of the county. I guess you've seen quite a bit of him this time, if he's into you for three hundred dollars."

Again Turner shrugged. "Closer to four hundred. Where'd you hear about that?"

"Amos Carter mentioned it. Any chance that could be the reason January's trumped up this holdup thing?"

"Who the hell can figure what he'd do!" Turner said heavily. "I've heard you say a couple of times that he's got no use for you, so he probably feels the same about me — being your brother. And then there's his card playing — hell, a ten-year-old kid could clean him! I've got so I don't like sitting in a game with him — it's too easy to take his money."

"Four hundred dollars," Frank murmured. "Ain't that a lot of cash for him to lose? Being sheriff's not the best-paying job around."

"Never thought much about it, but you're right. He always pays off, too — usually on his next trip into town."

"You mean he'll leave here after losing to you, then come back with the money to pay off later?"

"Yeh. May be a couple of weeks, or longer — sometimes even less — but he always squares up. If he didn't, I'd've turned him down when he came up to my table. I don't believe in letting myself get stung more'n once by the same bee."

"Sort of puzzles me where he'd get chunks of money like that to pay off —"

Turner nodded. "Done some wondering about that myself. Tom's sure got a Santy Claus somewhere that sweetens his poke when it's needful," he said, and then turned and crossed to the cot. Reaching under it, he procured a handkerchief tied into the shape of a small bag.

"Want you to keep this for me," he said, coming back to the front of the cage and passing the item to Frank. "There's some money in it, along with Pa's watch and Ma's wedding ring. Scared if I hang onto it here it'll end up in Tom January or Cheyenne Jones's pocket."

Frank thrust the packet inside his shirt. "I'll look after it," he said.

"Look after what?" a voice demanded from the doorway.

Garnett wheeled and faced January. Standing a step behind him was his deputy, Cheyenne Jones.

"Nothing that's any business of yours, Sheriff," Frank said coldly.

"Anything that goes on in my jail's my business," the sheriff said. In his early forties, January was a squat, heavily built man with ruddy skin and light eyes.

"Not always — and unless things've changed since I was here a time ago, the jail belongs to the town, and Amos Carter is the man running it."

January came slowly into the office area, a look of contempt on his broad face, and entered the cell corridor.

"Happens I'm the sheriff of the whole county, not just part of it, Mr. Bounty Hunter," he said. "That makes me the head honcho."

Jones, a lean, angular blond with small, darting eyes and a soaring ambition to succeed Tom January, closed in while maintaining that respectful step behind his superior.

"Whatever you say," Frank murmured, shrugging. "What I want to know is what kind of a ringer you're pulling on my brother."

The lawman's features darkened. "Ringer — hell! He's got hisself in a tight spot and he's going to answer for it!"

"You don't believe that any more than I do," Frank replied angrily. "He didn't have anything to do with the holdup — and you damn well know it! What are you up to, Tom? What's this all about?"

January's face grew even darker. "Don't you go jumping at me, Bounty Hunter, or by God I'll make you sorry you ever opened your trap!"

"And if you ever rough my brother up again, I'll bend my gun barrel over your thick head!" Frank shot back, equally angry.

January remained a silent, outraged figure for a long minute, and then abruptly he relaxed. A trace of a smile cracked his lips.

"Hell, there ain't no use in us yelling at each other — and you've got this all wrong. I'm just taking Turner up to Johnsburg for some questioning, that's all. Them two owlhoots he was palling around with claims he was in on that holdup. I expect he can prove he wasn't — and that'll be the end of it."

"He can do that right here, without going to Johnsburg —"

"Nope, he can't," January said bluntly. "In something like this he's got to appear in the regular court at the county seat. Them two others, Hoskins and Peters, and the fellow that got robbed'll be there, too. I reckon Turner'll be able to straighten it all out — if he ain't guilty."

"You think he is?" Frank asked, studying the lawman narrowly. It had grown steadily darker inside the jail, and Jones, dropping back to the desk in the office, struck a match to the lamp.

"Hell, I ain't no judge," January said. "I just go out and do the collaring and the bringing in. Ain't up to me to say whether he's guilty or not."

"Sure pleased to hear that, Sheriff," Frank said dryly. "That'll make Turner feel good — like for sure he is going to get a square deal. Me, too — but I aim to be there just the same to see that he does."

January's features tightened. "You riding up to Johnsburg with us?"

"Planning on it."

The lawman's attitude took an abrupt change. "Now, I don't want no trouble from you, Frank!" he said harshly. "You get that straight right now."

"Long as you treat Turner right you won't get any from me," Garnett said quietly. "And while we're talking, seems you owe him about four hundred dollars. I want you to pay him off before we leave. I'd feel better if it was stashed away at home."

January hawked, spat into the dry dust in a corner of the narrow hallway. "You'll have to wait. I ain't got that much on me. I'm good for it — Turner knows that. Don't you, Turner?"

"I reckon so — always have been," the older Garnett said from his cell. "But like my brother says, I'd like to get it now."

"Well, you'll just have to wait," the lawman snapped, and threw a sharp glance at Frank. "I'm aiming to ride out at first light in the morning. If you're wanting to come, you be here and ready."

"You can bank on it," Frank Garnett said as he watched January wheel and head for the door. Turning slightly, he nodded to Cheyenne Jones, utterly silent all during the time he was present. "Was nice talking to you, Deputy," he said with a sly grin.

Jones paused, started to voice an angry retort, and then thinking better of it, trailed off after his superior.

"You for certain going to Johnsburg with me?" Turner asked. He had moved back and was now sitting on the cot. Pale and haggard, he appeared to be in need of rest.

"I'll be right with you every foot of the way," Frank reassured him. "Big thing now is for you to get some sleep. That'll be a hard ride tomorrow —"

"Where you going now?"

"Over to the house to shave and clean up a bit, then to the restaurant to see Jenny."

Turner nodded. "Like for you to tell Darla not to worry none, that this'll come out all right."

Frank smiled grimly. "I expect to see to that personally. Anything you want?"

"Nope — nothing."

"I'll be seeing you later on — or in the morning for certain," Frank Garnett said as he crossed to the door and stepped out into the last of the daylight.

CHAPTER
FIVE

Garnett turned into the yard fronting the small house where he and his brother lived, noted that his horse had already been stabled in the shed behind the structure, and moved toward the door. At once an attractive but worn-looking woman came hurrying out to meet him.

"Frank!" she cried in a voice filled with relief as she threw her arms about him. "Thank God you're back! Did you see Turner? Amos said —"

"Just came from the jail, Darla," Garnett replied soberly, and then as she broke her embrace and they continued on up the board walk, added, "He's all right. Said for you not to worry."

"I — I can't help worrying," the woman said. "Having to stay there in that jail — and he's been sick —"

Garnett reached out ahead of her, pulled open the screen door for her to enter, and then followed her into the house. She had lit the lamps against the darkness, and the place was filled with the tempting smells of cooking. Pausing in the center of the small front room, he glanced about. His saddlebags and blanket roll were on a nearby chair — courtesy of Amos Carter, he assumed.

"Good to be home," he said after a few moments. "Realize that every time I come back."

"What will they do to Turner in Johnsburg?" Darla asked, breaking into his thoughts.

"Figuring everything will go the way it should, the judge'll turn him loose," Frank said, and let it drop there. He could have stated he feared some sort of frame-up on the part of Sheriff Tom January, but felt there was no point in increasing the woman's deep worry.

"Are you going with him?"

Garnett nodded. "Meeting him and the sheriff at the jail in the morning — first light," he replied, and taking up his blanket roll and saddlebags, crossed to the door leading into the room he occupied when in town.

"Got to clean up a bit — aim to do some checking around. I want to see what I can find out about this holdup January claims Turner was in on. I'd like to find a witness who'd swear he was somewhere else when that cattleman was being robbed."

"I thought of that — and so did Turner," Darla said wearily. "I had no luck, and Turner can't remember himself where he was at the time."

Frank considered that thoughtfully. "I'll do a bit of talking to him about that on the way to Johnsburg tomorrow — before he goes up before that judge. We didn't get much hashed out at the jail — January and his deputy showed up."

The woman's eyes snapped. "That — that man! And that bootlicker of his — Jones! They're at the bottom of this! The sheriff hates Turner because he always loses

30

money to him. And that's something else — there's something fishy about where he gets all that money to gamble with!"

Garnett came to attention. "Do you know anything for sure about it — something you've heard around the Jubilee?"

Darla nodded. "Been talk at the saloon all right. I've told Turner."

"Tell me," Garnett said bluntly.

"Well, some of the regulars that hang around and know the sheriff think he's got a lot of cash somewhere — cash that he maybe recovered but didn't turn in when he arrested some outlaw for a holdup. They figure he keeps it hid out and only uses it a bit at a time so folks won't get suspicious."

Frank nodded. It could be true — and it sounded like something Tom January would be guilty of. The lawman would have had to kill the outlaw — or outlaws — he'd apprehended, however, to eliminate any witnesses, and if —

Garnett's thoughts took a sudden turn; that could be the answer! It was possible that Turner knew the party — or parties — involved in a holdup, and that Tom January for some reason had come to fear that Turner was conscious of his secret, so the sheriff was taking steps to silence him.

Frank mulled these conclusions over in his mind and shrugged after a few moments. It was possible, of course, but it was pure guesswork — supposition, and he could think of no way to come up with proof of any sort.

"Probably all talk," he remarked absently.

Darla nodded. "Expect so, but folks all think it's plenty odd how the sheriff shows up every so often with a pocketful of cash."

"I reckon that does make a fellow wonder," Frank agreed, pulling off his jacket and beginning to remove his shirt. "Proving what some folks think's the truth won't help Turner, though, unless we can show that he knows about a holdup where January kept the money and that he's framing my brother to keep him from talking."

"That could be it," the woman murmured.

"I asked Turner when I was at the jail if he could come up with a reason why January would want him out of the way — said he couldn't think of one."

Darla shook her head and brushed at her eyes with the hem of the apron she was wearing. "There — there just has to be something, Frank!" she said in a desperate tone.

"I'm agreeing with that," Garnett said, and frowned. "Only thing — if January's set on keeping Turner from talking, I can't see him letting him stand up in front of a judge. If Turner knows something, that would be the time to say it."

"If he actually does know something —"

"Which maybe he doesn't. I'm starting to think there's something else at the bottom of this — and just as soon as I get to Johnsburg, I'm going to have a talk with those two outlaws, Hoskins and Peters, and see if I can come up with something."

"It seems our only hope," Darla admitted. "Do you want some supper? I've made beef stew, and I'm fixing to take some over to Turner for his supper. There's plenty if you'd like some."

Frank, tossing his shirt aside and tucking the handkerchief poke that Turner had entrusted to his care into one of the saddlebag pockets, nodded.

"Smells mighty good — and it'll be a real treat after my cooking . . . Like to clean up first."

"It will be ready any time you are," Darla said, and turned away.

An hour and a half later Frank Garnett was on McCurdy's main street, making his way along the nearly deserted sidewalk to the Home Restaurant, where Jenny Pittman worked as a combination waitress, cashier, and occasional cook. The business was owned by Jenny's elderly aunt, who relied on her niece for help in keeping the place going.

As Frank pulled open the door and entered, Jenny, serving a couple at a table along the side wall, glanced up. At once her lips parted into a glad smile, and Garnett felt his pulse quicken. She was pleased to see him — and that was an encouraging sign.

Moving on, he crossed to the back of the room and settled in the farthest corner. Jenny came to him at once, a cup of coffee for him in her hand.

"Sure good to see you," he said as she halted before him.

"I can say the same," she replied.

Not tall, and clad in a straight dress that did nothing for her well-developed figure, Jenny had dark hair, pale-blue eyes, and a pert nose that lent an aura of mischief to her expression.

"You've been gone a long time —"

Frank said, "Too long," and suddenly emboldened, added, "Sure hope you missed me as much as I did you."

Jenny smiled, exposing twin rows of small, white teeth. "My, how you speak up! If I answered that, I'd be giving away my secret — and a girl's supposed to keep that from —"

When she paused, Frank leaned forward. "What secret, and from who?"

Jenny's brows lifted to haughty arches. "Now, wouldn't you like to know!"

Garnett sighed heavily and settled back. "I would for a fact, because I was wondering all the way from Arkansas if you'd think about tying up — marrying me. I'm no big catch, and maybe you don't favor the way I make a living, but I —"

Jenny reached out and placed a finger against his lips to still his words. "You don't need to say things like that — it doesn't matter."

He frowned as she lowered her hand and sat down at the table. "That mean you'll do some thinking about it?"

"It means I'll marry you, Frank Garnett — no matter what you do for a living! I'm just puzzled why it took you so long to ask me."

34

Garnett rubbed the back of his neck. The skin on his face showed lighter where he had shaved off the whiskers that had turned away the sun.

"Kept thinking you'd not like me being, well — a bounty hunter. Most folks don't have much use for my kind."

"Why? It's a job — a sort of a lawman job."

"That's the way I see it, but there are plenty who look at it in a different way."

She smiled. "I doubt if that's ever really bothered you."

"No, it sure hasn't — and I can make more money doing it than I could doing anything else. The reward I'll be getting for the outlaw I just brought in will build up what I've got stashed away to more'n two thousand dollars. I guess that's what gave me the sand to ask you to marry me — having enough cash to make a good start."

"That's wonderful, Frank — but that doesn't matter either. It's only us, the two of us making a life together, that does."

Garnett had the urge to reach out, grasp Jenny by the shoulders, and drawing her close, kiss her soundly. But the elderly couple at the nearby table was watching, and anyone outside on the walk or in the street could see through the window.

"Got some things to do," he said then, reluctantly restraining himself. "You know about Turner —"

Jenny shook her head. "It's a shame. Nobody thinks he had anything to do with that holdup."

"That's how I see it — and I believe him. I'm riding up to Johnsburg with him and the sheriff in the morning and see that he gets cleared of the charges that January, for some reason, has trumped up against him."

A slight frown clouded Jenny's brow. It disappeared quickly. "How long will you be gone?"

"Shouldn't take long — three, maybe four days. When I get back I'd sure like to continue this talk we're having."

"We can do that tonight after I close up," Jenny said. "I'm not letting you get cold feet again — we're going to make plans and keep them! Now sit right there and drink your coffee. I'll be locking up in an hour or so — then we'll talk."

Garnett, despite the seriousness of the situation involving his brother, grinned happily. The doubts and fears regarding his relationship with Jenny Pittman that had plagued his mind for months had disappeared completely. All he had dared hope and dream for was going to come true.

"Yes'm," he said in mock servility. "I'll sit right here — just like you ordered."

CHAPTER
SIX

Frank Garnett was up and about well before first light that next morning, although he had stayed up past midnight making plans for the future with Jenny.

But the few hours' sleep had benefitted him, as usual, and now, in the dim light of the shed behind the house that was used as a stable, he was throwing his gear into place on the bay gelding and making things ready for the journey. Everything had been settled with Jenny; as soon as he returned from Johnsburg and the business of Turner's alleged crime was cleared to everyone's satisfaction, they would marry and set out for St. Louis on a honeymoon.

On the way home from Jenny's earlier, he had dropped by the jail to see if there was anything his brother needed for the trip — as well as to tell him of his good fortune with Jenny — but when he entered, Marshal Carter had warned him that Turner had finally managed to go to sleep, and suggested that he not be disturbed.

"Was sort of worked up all evening," the lawman had said. "But he's right pleased that you'll be riding along with him. Said he was real anxious to see that judge and straighten everything out. He's aiming to marry that gal, Darla, when it's over."

Frank had grinned. "We can make it a double wedding. Jenny Pittman and me — we're getting married, too, when I get back."

Amos Carter nodded approvingly. "Best thing you boys could do. Them's mighty nice gals. If Turner wakes up, I'll tell him."

"I'll be obliged," Garnett had said. "You be here when we ride out in the morning?"

"Ain't knowing that. Sheriff just said for me to spend the night with the prisoner. Expect I'll be going home and getting myself some sleep when him and the deputy shows up."

"Well, if I don't see you in the morning, I will when we get back," Frank had said, then continued on his way.

Gear in place and horse ready, Garnett swung up into the saddle, and cutting the bay about, headed into the lane that led to the street. Darla was not awake, having taken his suggestion to say her farewells to Turner the previous evening so as to avoid further confusion at the time of departure. He would have liked to tell the woman about Jenny and him, but under the circumstances it was best that he wait. More than likely the two women would get together while he and Turner were gone, anyway.

The muffled crack of a gunshot came to Frank and brought a quick frown to his face. It was not possible to determine the direction from which the sound had come — the inside of a house or building not far away, he was certain. A sudden wave of apprehension swept through Garnett as a grim possibility came to mind. The jail — Turner!

Jamming spurs into the bay, Garnett rushed the remaining distance to where the structure stood. Three horses were at the hitch rack in the front, and lamplight was filtering through the dusty windows. Leaving his saddle in a hurried leap, he ran to the doorway.

Frank drew up short, the cutting odor of burnt gunpowder assailing his nostrils. The shot had come from inside the jail, as he'd feared. Hand dropping to the pistol on his hip, he stepped up into the doorway and entered. Tom January, holding his weapon, wheeled to face him. The ever-present but wordless Cheyenne Jones was an arm's length beyond. In the corridor lay a man in a dusty frock coat. It could only be Turner. Shock and fear and anxiety rolled through Garnett as he hurried to his brother's side.

"What happened here?" he demanded in a low, savage voice.

"Can see, can't you?" January snapped. "That brother of yours got hisself a gun somehow. Tried to fire on me when I come for him — had to shoot. Can ask the deputy there if that ain't how it was."

"I wouldn't believe him any sooner than I would you," Garnett said, kneeling beside Turner and feeling for a pulse.

There was none. The bullet, entering his brother's body just below the left shoulder, had killed quickly. Grief welled up in Frank Garnett in a choking wave, and for a brief time he remained motionless while a thousand memories, good and bad, of his life with Turner flooded through his mind. And then cold hatred took over.

He started to rise, then saw the pistol on the floor beside Turner's outflung hand. Picking it up, he examined it closely and then drew himself erect.

"This the gun you're claiming Turner had?" he demanded.

"That's it," January said.

Frank shook his head. "Little hard to believe. It belonged to Lige Webster, an outlaw I brought in yesterday. It was hanging on a peg behind Carter's desk when I dropped by here a bit after midnight. How in the hell could my brother, being in a cell, get it?"

"Well, he sure in hell did!" January said hotly. "I expect somebody slipped it to him."

Garnett, maintaining control of his temper with difficulty, said, "Who?"

"Could've been that woman of his. She come here, bringing him some grub —"

"Wasn't her," Frank cut in flatly. "I was here after she left. Gun was still on that peg."

The lawman shrugged indifferently. "I reckon it was somebody else then — maybe old Amos."

"Not him either," Garnett said. "I know Amos Carter — and so do you. He's an honest man — he'd never pull something like that. Where is he?"

"Home sleeping, I expect."

"You send him away when you got here?"

"Yeh, matter of fact I did. Had him stand watch over the prisoner like he's supposed to do, then told him to go on home when Cheyenne and me come."

"Which means he wasn't around when you claim Turner pulled the gun on you —"

"You saying I'm a liar about this?" January cut in, face darkening. "Don't you go accusing me of something — you damned bounty hunter! I ain't no two-bit owlhoot that you can plug in the back!"

Garnett's eyes flashed momentarily, and then taking a firm grip on himself, he shifted his attention to the deputy.

"Did you give that gun to Turner and tell him to make a run for it — that he was being framed? That it?"

Cheyenne Jones scowled. "No sir, I never give him no gun! Wasn't me — was somebody else —"

"I figure he never did have it," Garnett said quietly, coming back to Tom January. "My guess is that you wanted him dead, and you shot him down and dropped Webster's gun on the floor beside him to back up your lie."

The sheriff's color deepened even further. His mouth worked spasmodically, and his eyes narrowed into small slits.

"You — you saying I murdered your brother?" January's voice was high-pitched, strained.

"I'm telling you what it looks like to me — and what it'll look like to a U.S. Marshal," Garnett replied evenly. He was deliberately baiting the man, hoping to anger him and cause him to blurt out words that would reveal why he had killed Turner, and thus brand himself the murderer. And with Cheyenne Jones present, there would be a witness to all that was said.

"From what I've learned, I think you had something against my brother — something that has to do with all that money you keep showing up with. My hunch is that he knew where you were getting it."

"Damn you — I ain't putting up with no talk like that!" January yelled. "Turner didn't know nothing about —"

The lawman's voice faltered, then faded into silence as he realized he was getting himself into a corner.

"Maybe," Frank said quietly. "But I reckon the marshal can get to the bottom of it real quick when I tell him what happened —"

"You ain't telling nobody nothing!" January snarled and whipped up the pistol he was holding for a quick shot.

The break in Tom January's expression betrayed him doubly; it convinced Garnett that the sheriff was lying when he claimed Turner had tried to escape, and proved that he was in such desperate straits that he was willing to kill again in order to silence an accuser.

Frank Garnett, never off guard in like moments, had been alert for any change in the man and reacted instantly. His arm swept up as he rocked to one side. The bone-handled weapon he carried appeared magically in his hand. Its shocking blast came a fragment of time ahead of that of January's.

The lawman was slammed back against the wall from the impact of the heavy bullet striking him from such close range. He hung there briefly, and then, as powder smoke boiled through the small jail area, his lifeless body sagged forward and fell to the floor.

"God in heaven!" Cheyenne Jones said in a breathless sort of voice. "You've done killed the sheriff!"

CHAPTER
SEVEN

Garnett, pistol hanging at his side, slowly drew himself erect. "He was trying to kill me, Deputy, don't forget that," he said in a low, taut voice.

Cheyenne Jones nodded. "That's for sure. Already had his gun out. Don't know what, but there's been something wrong with the sheriff lately."

Frank Garnett shrugged, replaced the spent cartridge in the cylinder of his weapon, and slid it back into its holster.

"It have something to do with my brother?"

The deputy had crossed to where January lay. Unpinning the lawman's star, he dropped it into his own vest pocket and then, picking up the dead man's gun, turned to the desk at the back of the room.

"Don't know about that either," he said, dropping the weapon into a drawer. "Sure could be, but Tom's been mighty close-mouthed . . . I reckon this sort of puts me in charge."

Frank looked closely at Jones. "Expect it does."

The last curls of gunpowder smoke had drifted through the open doorway, and now the sharp, cool air of early morning filled the room. Faint sounds were coming from the town, indicating that many of its residents were up and beginning a new day.

"Kind of hate doing this, Frank, but I'll have to lock you up —"

At the deputy's words, Garnett's jaw hardened. "What the hell for? You saw what happened."

"Sure — sure! You done what you had to. Was no choice, but locking you up's something I have to do. The law says you've got to be held till somebody higher up hears the story and decides it was self-defense and turns you loose. It won't be no problem — I seen everything. It's what they call a formality."

Garnett nodded, agreeing that it was a matter of procedures. But he was willing to go along with it only so far.

"Who'll you get to hear the story? I'm not about to lay around in a cell for more'n a day or so."

"A U.S. deputy marshal — he's riding in today. Was coming to meet with the sheriff. Name's John Crissman. You can tell him what happened."

"You tell him," Garnett said. "You're proof that January was going to kill me — I just beat him to pulling the trigger. Killed my brother, too."

"I'll handle it," Cheyenne said. His voice had taken on an authoritative quality, and he was now wearing two guns — his own and Lige Webster's, recovered from the floor where Frank Garnett had dropped it. "Now I best get ahold of Leo Thompson, have him take these two dead men over to his undertaking parlor, so if you'll just get in one of them cells —"

"I'll look after my brother," Garnett said.

Jones frowned and brushed at his jaw. "Ain't sure I can do that, Frank. You're supposed to be locked up, not out running around loose."

"I won't be — I'll be seeing to Turner's burying. When that's done I'll turn myself in to you."

The deputy gave that thought. "Well, I reckon that'll have to do. I sure ain't about to try drawing against you to make you do what I say. You give me your word?"

Garnett nodded, and washing all else from his mind except the bitterness and grief that the death of Turner imposed on him, he turned, knelt, and lifting his brother's frail body, cradled it in his arms as if it were that of a child as he carried it some distance to the building housing the town's mortuary.

The rear door was locked, but after several insistent raps with the toe of his boot it opened, and Thompson, a small, quiet-faced man greeted him with a fixed, professional smile. His brows lifted instantly when he recognized Frank.

"Mr. Garnett! I —"

"This is my brother," Frank cut in bruskly, and pushing past the man, laid Turner's body on an oblong table. "I want the best coffin you've got — and I want him ready to bury in a couple of hours."

"Certainly," Thompson said, and glanced to the door as Cheyenne Jones, the body of Tom January hung over a shoulder, entered. Motioning for the deputy to make use of a second table, the undertaker brought his attention back to Frank.

"That don't give me much time. There'll be the grave to dig, and folks to notify, and the preacher —"

"You take care of the grave part, I'll get in touch with the folks I want to have around — and don't bury him next to that one," Garnett added, jerking a thumb at January.

Thompson frowned, looked again at the body Jones had brought in. "That the sheriff?" he asked in an awed tone, and then added, "What happened?"

"The deputy can tell you," Frank replied, and started for the door.

"Everything'll be just like you want," he heard the mortician say. "I'll send the carriage over to your place for you when we're ready."

Garnett made no reply as he continued on to the street. He halted there in the early dawn, the town steadily coming alive around him. With the heat of violence behind him for the first time since he'd stepped into the dimly lit jail and seen Turner's lifeless body, he felt the full impact of his brother's death.

They had been close — more so than average — for many years, with a loyalty and interdependence that nothing, from the time they were small boys until the present day, could shake. Each had seen to the welfare and care of the other, and it had been share and share alike — or not at all.

It was all over now. Turner was gone — out of this world, victim not of the ravaging wounds a terrible war had inflicted upon him, but of a greedy, cowardly man's fear. That the killer had paid full price for his act was only small comfort; Turner was gone and nothing could bring him back.

He had to break the news to Darla — a chore he did not relish. Dead men as such, even those slain by his own hand, had little effect upon his emotions. But Turner was blood kin and that changed everything. Swallowing hard, Garnett returned to the jail, mounted his horse, and rode back to the house.

Darla had just awakened and was in the kitchen making coffee when he opened the door and moved to the center of the room. The woman, a frown darkening her lovely face, stared at him questioningly, and then as realization burst in her, she hurried to him.

"It's Turner!" she cried in a rising voice. "Something's happened to him!"

"He's dead," Frank said flatly, making the moment no easier for her than it was for him. "Tom January did it. He's dead, too."

Darla clung to him for a long moment, sobbing wildly while he tried to comfort her, and then as a knock came on the door he pushed her gently aside, and struggling with his own composure, turned and drew back the panel.

It was Amos Carter. The aging lawman, hat in hand, came into the room as Garnett stepped back and allowed him to enter.

"Just heard what happened," he said. "Sure am mighty sorry, Frank — ma'am. There something I can do?"

Garnett shook his head, frowning. "Obliged to you, Amos, but no . . . Where'd you hear about it? Only been a few minutes."

"It's all over town," Carter said. "I reckon it was Thompson and the deputy that spread the word. Run into him at the jail. He's making loud talk about you plugging the sheriff."

Frank shrugged. "After he'd shot Turner and tried to frame him with Lige Webster's six-shooter. I called his hand on it."

The town marshal nodded. "See the deputy is packing that gun now — got it stuck in his belt . . . You in any trouble over shooting January?"

"No. Was him that made the first move. Cheyenne was right there and saw everything. Said he'd tell the deputy that's coming in today how it was — that I had to use my gun. Expect he'll explain how Turner got shot, too. The sheriff claimed he was trying to escape."

"Ain't nobody'd believe that," Carter said. "Cheyenne's sure mighty important right now! He's even put on Tom's star. Says that, long as he's the acting sheriff, he figures he ought to be wearing the badge."

"That's how he'd look at it," Garnett said, and glanced at Darla. She had recovered her poise somewhat and had turned to the stove for distraction. "I guess he's finally got what he's been after — January's job."

"Something he can only keep till election time comes around," Carter said.

"For sure . . . Like to ask a favor, Amos."

"Just you name it."

"Pass the word to Turner's friends — you know who they are better than I do. I'd like for them to be at the

49

burying — a couple of hours from now. Want to have that reverend fellow from the Methodist church, too."

"Thompson'll see to him being there. He calls the priest when the funeral's for a Catholic and the reverend if it ain't."

"My pa and ma were church people. Only right that a preacher say some words over Turner."

"Sure — just you leave everything to me," Carter said, and opened the door to leave. "You've got some more company," he continued, and moved aside to let Jenny Pittman enter.

Features grave, the girl stepped up to Frank and wordlessly threw her arms about his neck. He gathered her in, held her close as grief once more rocked him, and then as Darla came forward he surrendered her to the older woman.

"I'm so sorry," Jenny murmured as they embraced.

Darla could only smile wearily, and then breaking down again, moved off into the adjoining bedroom and closed the door. Jenny turned back to Frank.

"Meant that for you, too —"

He shrugged, shook his head. "It's tough, got to admit that. Turner and me — well, we've been looking out for each other for a lot of years. I'm kicking myself for letting them keep him in that jail. He'd be alive right now if I'd done what I ought to."

"You can't blame yourself, Frank — not for that. There's no way you could have known that the sheriff —"

"January — damn him to hell — him being a part of it should've been enough to warn me! He was a snake, something a man couldn't trust in no way, shape, or form — the kind that gives lawmen a bad name!"

"It'll do no good to whip yourself over what happened," Jenny said reprovingly, and taking him by the arm, she guided him to the kitchen table and pressed him into a chair. Procuring two cups from a nearby shelf, she filled them with coffee from the pot on the stove.

"Is it true that — that you shot and killed the sheriff?" Jenny asked hesitantly, a note of concern in her voice.

Garnett, feeling better some after having voiced the fury bottled up within him, took a sip of the strong, black liquid. "Yeah, it's true — but there'll be no trouble. The deputy's going to explain what happened to some U.S. deputy marshal that's due in this afternoon, tell him that I didn't have a choice. That will clear me. Have to wait in jail till the marshal gets here."

"Jones is locking you up?" Jenny's eyes opened wide with alarm.

Frank's shoulders lifted, then fell. "Times like this it's customary — and I want that marshal to clear me. The law's got nothing against my name now, and I aim to keep it that way. Don't fret — it'll be all right."

Jenny smiled. "If you say so —"

"I do — and there's no reason why we can't go ahead with our plans in a couple of days."

"I'll be ready when you are," the girl said, then got to her feet. "I best look in on Darla, see if she needs any help."

"I'd appreciate that," Garnett said. "Same as I'd be obliged if you'd go to the cemetery with us for the burying."

"Of course," Jenny said, and after pausing to kiss him lightly on the cheek, hurried on into the bedroom.

CHAPTER
EIGHT

True to his word, the undertaker had arrived in a curtained carriage to convey Frank Garnett and his party of two women to the cemetery when all was ready. Arriving there, Frank had found a dozen or so mourners, including Amos Carter and the Methodist minister, awaiting them beside the open grave.

As directed, Thompson had selected a site on a bleak and barren slope, far from the spot where a man was hollowing out another grave for Sheriff Tom January.

The words spoken over Turner Garnett by the minister were few but choice, gleaned from conversations with Amos Carter and other individuals who had known him, and when it was all over, Frank had thanked those who'd attended and ridden back to the house with Jenny and Darla. Then, after settling with Thompson for services rendered and assuring both women there was no need to worry, he returned to the jail and turned himself in to Deputy Jones, as promised. Now, as the shadows began to lengthen and the six or eight hours he'd been locked in a cell started to pall, he fell to pacing restlessly back and forth in his barred cage.

"Deputy!" he called finally, halting at the hinged grill that formed the door.

Jones, evidently sitting at the desk, responded indifferently. "Yeh?"

"Where the hell's that marshal? You said he was coming today."

A chair squeaked, there was the scrape and shuffling of boots, and a moment later Cheyenne Jones sauntered into the cell corridor. Hat pushed to the back of his head, he had Frank's pistol in his hand and was toying with it.

"This sure is some shooting iron," he said admiringly. "Got the sight filed down and the front half of the trigger guard's been cut off. And that there trigger — why, a man could shoot this gun just by blowing on it!"

Garnett was frowning. "Best you be a mite careful with it, Deputy," he warned. "Could hurt yourself."

"Oh, I reckon not," Jones replied loftily, his tone reflecting the exalted state of importance that he had acquired since the death of the sheriff. "There ain't no straw sticking out of my collar — I been fooling with guns maybe long as you have."

"Could be," Garnett said. "What about that marshal?"

"Ought to be here in a bit," Cheyenne said, wheeling slowly and heading back into the office area. "Seen him down the street a few minutes ago — had a little talk with him. Mighty fine fellow."

Garnett swore distractedly. "Let's get him over here — I want out of this damned cage."

54

"Just hold your horses some, he'll —" the deputy's voice broke off. "That's him acoming now," he finished.

Frank heaved a sigh of relief. He'd been in the cell for only a few hours, but it was a maddening experience. He understood now why some outlaws preferred to shoot it out at the time of capture rather than face a term in prison.

The thump of boot heels reached Garnett, after which he heard a brief exchange of greetings between Jones and the federal lawman, whose name, he recalled, was John Crissman. Judging by the talk between the two men, it appeared they were not acquainted, nor had there been a conversation earlier on the street as Cheyenne Jones had claimed. But it didn't matter — let the deputy have his bit of glory, Frank thought. All that mattered was his being freed from the cage he was in.

The two lawmen, their voices now lowered, talked for several minutes, during which time Garnett's impatience grew steadily. Finally the mumbling ceased and the marshal, followed by Deputy Jones, entered the corridor.

Crissman, a sharp-faced, intense-looking man in his late fifties, wearing a dusty brown suit and a narrow-brimmed hat, stepped up close to the bars of Garnett's cell. There was a hard set to his features, and his eyes were bright agates.

"Going to be a pleasure to see you swing, mister," he said in a voice that quivered with anger. "Nobody murders a lawman in my district and gets away with it!"

Frank stared at the marshal in disbelief. After a moment he shook his head. "You've got it wrong,

Marshal. Tom January brought it on himself — the deputy'll tell you that."

"He told me you murdered the sheriff in cold blood," Crissman said flatly. "Said Tom had your brother locked up, but had to shoot him when he tried to escape. Then you showed up and killed Tom — killed him for doing his duty."

Garnett's wintery gaze settled on Jones. "You damned double-crossing liar," he said in a low voice that carried its own threat. "It was not that way and you know it!"

Cheyenne Jones shrugged. He was now carrying Frank's .45, the weapon's bone handle riding a bit high in a holster that was too small for it.

"Can cuss me all you want, bounty hunter," he said. "What I expected — but you murdered the sheriff."

"Not murder," Frank retorted. "There's no truth in that yarn you gave the marshal."

"What are you claiming's the truth?" Crissman asked.

"January had something against my brother and was framing him. He figured to take him to Johnsburg — so he claimed — to face a judge. I was going along just to make sure he'd get there and be treated square. We were to leave at first light this morning. When I got here I found Turner — my brother — laying dead on the floor."

"January claimed Turner was trying to escape. I knew better — knew my brother wouldn't try it. First off, he was a sick man, and second, the charge the sheriff had trumped up against him was a lie, and any

56

judge he'd stand up before was sure to turn him loose. I started asking January questions about it — about what he was trying to do, and why. I must've been getting close to the truth, because he lost his head and started to throw down on me — still had his gun in his hand after shooting Turner. I drew and got him before he could get me."

"That's a mighty fancy tale," Crissman said. "But you're wasting your wind, bounty hunter. I wouldn't take your word against a lawman's if you was to swear on a stack of bibles ten foot high!"

"That's just the way it was," Frank said evenly. "The deputy there said he'd tell it to you straight — just like I did — if I'd let him lock me up. Can see now it was a trick."

"How else was I going to get your gun and put you in a cell for the marshal?" Jones asked, gesturing helplessly with his hands. "Knew I didn't stand a chance against a killer like you."

"You lied me into here," Frank said. "You've been wanting Tom January's job, and you figured hanging a murder charge on me and locking me up would get it for you."

"Something wrong with that?" Crissman said. "I'm taking my hat off to the man. Admits he couldn't take you head-on, being the gun slick you are, so he done the next best thing — outsmarted you."

"No, being smart had nothing to do with it. Being a double-crossing liar looking out for himself did —"

"I ain't listening, Garnett. You're blowing for nothing. I'll take a lawman's word over that of a blood-sucker like you seven days a week — no matter what . . . Now you settle down in there. I've got some business to 'tend to for the rest of the day, then tomorrow we'll head for Capital City. I aim to stand you up in front of a judge there who'll —"

Crissman paused as the sound of someone entering the jail reached him. Amos Carter appeared in the corridor's entrance. Frowning, the old lawman glanced about and then nodded to Crissman.

"You the U.S. marshal?"

John Crissman nodded. "Yeh — deputy marshal. Who're you?"

"Name's Amos Carter. I'm the town marshal. This here's my jail," he added, throwing a hard look at Cheyenne Jones.

Crissman nodded. "Glad you showed up. I'll be obliged if you'll continue to hold this prisoner for me. I'll be riding north with him in the morning."

"Why? He was supposed to be turned loose."

"Hardly," the federal lawman said. "He'll stand trial and swing for the murder of Sheriff Tom January."

Amos Carter swore loudly, turned a glowering face to Jones. "This is your doing, ain't it, Deputy? You know dang well Frank didn't murder the sheriff. Was self-defense, pure and simple."

"You know that for a fact?" Crissman said, his tone skeptical. "You see it with your own eyes?"

Carter rubbed at the whiskers on his jaw. He had neglected to shave that morning because of the excitement and activity.

"Well, no," he replied haltingly. "Was Frank there that told me how it was —"

"You mean the prisoner — Frank Garnett?"

"Who the hell else would we be talking about?" Carter demanded testily. "Sure I'm meaning him."

Crissman smiled humorlessly. "You think he'd just up and say he'd murdered Tom January?"

"He would if he had," the old lawman declared. "I know Frank Garnett. He don't lie — not about anything."

"Always a first time," the federal marshal said indifferently, moving away from the cell. He paused in front of Carter. "I'll remind you, you're an officer of the law and you're responsible for this prisoner. I expect to find him here when I come for him in the morning."

"He'll be here," Cheyenne Jones assured Crissman, holding up the keys to Garnett's cell for the federal man to see, and then dropping them into a pocket. "I aim to look after him myself — seeing that nothing happens . . . You might as well go on home, Amos."

"The hell I will!" Carter exploded. "This here's my jail and I reckon I'll do what I please!"

John Crissman moved for the doorway. "Likely a good idea, Deputy," he said, hesitating. "I ain't so sure about your town marshal. Any lawman worth his salt will side with another lawman no matter what the score is — good or bad. I'll just leave it all up to you to take care of things — and have my prisoner ready and waiting when I come for him in the morning."

CHAPTER
NINE

Carter muttered under his breath as he watched Crissman pass on through the office part of the jail and step out into the open. Jones delayed briefly, and then, patting the cell keys in his pocket as if to remind both Carter and Garnett of their location, headed for the door also.

"So long, boys, I'll be back later," he said. "I'm going over to the Jubilee for a couple of drinks."

"You can go straight to hell, far as I'm concerned!" Amos Carter shot back angrily, and then brought his attention back to Frank. "That stinking, lying bastard — I'm going to —"

"I don't want you trying to help me," Garnett broke in. "I mean that, Amos."

The raging anger at Jones's duplicity had ebbed quickly, and Frank was now coolly facing his problem. What was done was done; he'd let himself be played for a sucker and it was up to him, and him alone, to figure a way out of the trouble he was in.

"What's that?" Carter said, frowning.

"Said I don't want you getting yourself mixed up in this. That's a federal marshal you'd be crossing, not to mention Cheyenne, who'll nail you to the wall if you give him half a chance."

"Maybe," Amos conceded, staring off through the open doorway. "But hell-a'mighty, I just can't stand around and let them two railroad you to the gallows!"

"I'm not ready to swing yet," Frank said. "Soon as we get through talking, I want you to get out of here and stay out — savvy?"

Carter again scrubbed at his whiskers. "Sure, but I don't see —"

"Already told you I don't want you around — I can't have them blaming you for something that might happen. Now listen, have you sent those papers for the reward on Lige Webster yet?"

"Got them about ready. Was going to put them on the mail coach tomorrow."

"I want you to change something. Have them send the reward to Jenny, at the restaurant."

"Can easily do that —"

"I'd appreciate it. And I'd like another favor. Go by and tell Jenny and Darla what's happened — they're both expecting me to be turned loose. I don't want either one of them coming by here."

Carter nodded. "For the same reason you don't want me hanging around — you're scared they might get blamed if you come up with a way to get out of this jail."

Frank smiled. "That's it. Just tell them to sit tight, that they'll hear from me sooner or later — if I pull it off."

"You got something in mind?"

"Not yet, but I'll be watching for a chance. Could be I'll have to wait until Crissman heads for Capital City with me. He won't make it — at least not with me. The way he's got it fixed, I'd not stand a chance before any judge — especially this one he's taking me to up there."

"And that two-bit Cheyenne — he'll lie right down to his boot heels to back him . . . Say, ain't that your gun he's wearing?"

"It is. Appears he's got me dead and buried already."

"Sure does," the old marshal agreed with a grim smile. "Same as him taking Tom January's star . . . Getting dark in here," he added, pointing to the lamp bracketed on the wall. "You want some light?"

"Let it go — leave everything just as it is. Remember Cheyenne told you to go on home, that he'd see to everything. Best you take him at his word — it'll keep you in the clear. Now Amos, if I don't see you again for a time, I want you to know I'm obliged for all you did for Turner and me — and for the women, too."

"Ain't nothing you wouldn't've done for me," Carter replied. "I'd like to say I'm mighty proud to be your friend, and I'm sure hoping things'll turn out for the best."

"Expect they will. When you talk to Jenny, say that I don't want her to fret, that I'll be fine."

"I'll do that. You real sure there ain't nothing else I can do for you?"

"Nothing — just get out of here and stay away. So long."

"So long," Carter answered, and making his way to the doorway through the half dark, stepped out into the closing night.

For a time Frank Garnett remained as he had been, leaning against the front bars of his cell. It would have been easy to ask Amos Carter for a gun, and the old lawman, despite his sense of obligation to his oath and the warning from John Crissman, likely would have complied.

But Garnett could not bring himself to involve Carter and subject him to the repercussions it undoubtedly would bring. It was best he go it alone, just as he always had — relying on no one else, and thereby creating no problems for others.

He hoped Jenny would understand and not make any attempt to see him. She had not trusted Cheyenne Jones from the start, he recalled, and it would be like her to want to help. The same applied to Darla; she too would be willing to assist in any way that she could — but he wanted none of it. If he could manage an escape while still in the McCurdy jail, he wanted no hint of blame to fall upon either of the women, or Amos Carter.

Voices sounded in the yard fronting the jail. Immediately Frank stepped back to the cot and stretched out on it, feigning sleep. Shortly he heard Cheyenne Jones cursing the darkness and Amos Carter for not leaving a lamp burning in the office. Then came the scrape of a chair being pushed aside, followed by the scratch of a match being struck, and then the sudden glow of yellow lamplight flooded the corridor.

"Best I take a look-see at my prisoner," the voice of the deputy, firm with importance, came to Garnett.

The cell filled with light as the lawman, holding a lamp above his head and followed by someone Frank, looking through barely slitted eyes, did not recognize, stepped in close. Jones stood for a brief time staring at Garnett's motionless shape, and then turned back to the office.

"Sleeping!" he said in a marveling tone. "That jasper's got the guts of an army mule! Going to be took to his own hanging tomorrow, and he just lays around and sleeps!"

Whoever it was with the deputy laughed and said, "Well, I reckon there ain't a hell of a lot else a man can do when he's sweating time out in the jug."

"Expect you're right," Cheyenne said, laughing too. "About time I was feeding him, however. I'll fetch some grub — don't want nobody saying I didn't treat him right while he was locked up."

The men departed, but the lamp on the desk continued to shed its light through most of the jail. He knew Jones would return soon with supper for him. If Frank was to be afforded an opportunity for escape from his cell, it would be now; otherwise, he would have to hope for a chance while he was in the company of John Crissman — and U.S. deputy marshals, being cautious and experienced lawmen, were not easily tricked.

Frank started to rise, hands flat on the cot. His hopes surged as he felt the inch-square metal pieces that made up his bed. At once he came to his feet, and turning to the cot, tested each one of the strips until he found one that was slightly loose. Grasping it with both hands, he pulled it free and stepped back. A hard grin split his lips. It wasn't much of a weapon, but it would do.

He finished just in time. He had hardly spread the thin blanket over the slats again, and was stretched out to formulate a plan, when he heard the deputy and his friend enter the jail.

"— The sheriff was living high on the money he took off them outlaws, so Crissman told me," Cheyenne Jones was saying. "That's what brought the marshal here — was aiming to collar Tom and take him in."

"Guess you could say it was just as good he got his-self killed —"

"Yeh, I reckon you could say that," Jones replied. "This here won't take long. Soon as he's done eating, I'll lock up the place and we can head for Minnie's."

"Can't you just leave his grub?"

"And give him something to use for a weapon — like a knife or maybe a fork? Nope, you don't take no chances with a jasper like Garnett."

The deputy was entering the corridor. Halting in the darkness, he called back to his companion.

"Jase — bring that lamp in here — and hold this damn tray while I get the door open."

Jase appeared immediately with the lamp, and hesitating uncertainly, finally set the light on the floor and took the tray from the deputy. Jones then inserted the key into the cell's lock and pulled open the grill, keeping his attention on Garnett, who evidently had been awakened by the arrival of the two men and was now sitting up.

"Here's your grub," the lawman said, taking the tray from Jase and stepping to the cage.

Garnett's response was immediate. "The hell with it!" he snarled. "I don't want nothing from you."

Jones shrugged. "Suit yourself, mister!" he snapped, and with both hands gripping the tray, started to turn.

Frank Garnett came off the cot with the speed of a striking rattler. He swung the slat he was holding with all the fury-driven force he could muster. It caught the deputy across the bridge of his nose, cracking the bone. In that same instant of time, he crashed full into the lawman, who, howling with pain, slammed into the side of the cell, rebounded, and sank to the floor. Reaching down, Frank recovered his bone-handled pistol from the deputy — noting as he did that Jones had also appropriated his belt and holster. As he started to release the buckle, Jase, who had been paralyzed momentarily by the swift turn of events, pivoted and moved for the door.

"Hold it!" Garnett snapped.

Jase halted in mid-stride, eyes on Frank, who beckoned to him. The man obeyed instantly, evidently expecting the worst. He received only a small measure of what he had anticipated. As he walked up, Garnett clubbed him solidly on the side of the head and dropped him flat to the floor, alongside the unconscious Cheyenne Jones.

Hastily removing his belt from the deputy and strapping it on, Frank holstered his weapon and went to work gagging and securely trussing the two men with strips of cloth obtained by ripping up the blanket on the cot. When that was done, Garnett relieved Jase of the weapon he carried, threw it into a far corner of the corridor, and closing the cell door, locked it.

Turning down the lamp, he departed by the front door, which he also locked. After tossing the keys into nearby brush, Frank headed for his house.

CHAPTER
TEN

The house was dark as Garnett turned into the yard, but he doubted that Darla had already retired. Moving up to the door, he tried the latch. Finding it unfastened, he entered.

"Darla —" he called softly, lighting the lamp.

"Here." The reply came from the bedroom. "That you, Frank?" she continued, and shortly appeared. Fully clothed, the woman had been sitting or lying on the bed in the dark. "I — I'm glad they turned you loose."

"They didn't," he said, hurrying into the side room where he had left his gear.

Darla was silent for a long moment. Then, "You broke out — escaped?"

He nodded as he took up his saddlebags and blanket roll. "Left Jones and some friend of his tied up in my cell. Figure I've got maybe a couple of hours' start before they work loose."

Darla turned at once to the stove. "I'll fix some food — don't have much in the house, but it'll get you by for a day or so . . . Where will you go?"

Garnett paused. He hadn't given that thought as yet. "North," he said after a bit. "I'll get up close to the

Canadian border, lay low till this blows over. Then I aim to come back and make Cheyenne Jones own up to the truth."

"You can't do that now?"

"Not with Crissman around. He's the U.S. deputy marshal that's figuring on taking me to Capital City and swinging me from a hanging tree. Think I found out why Tom January killed Turner. Seems the sheriff didn't get around to turning in the money he took off some outlaws — was keeping it for himself. Crissman was on his way here to arrest January —"

"But why would he — the sheriff — shoot —" the woman's voice broke and she looked away.

"Turner knew about it, I guess."

"We asked him if it was something like that that had gotten him thrown into jail. He said he couldn't think of anything he'd done that would have angered the sheriff," Darla reminded Frank.

"I know. Either it had slipped his mind or he actually didn't know — but Tom January thought he did, and he didn't want any witness talking to Crissman when he got here." Garnett paused. "Galls me when I think there was no need for Turner to die, none at all, but that damn Tom January and —"

Frank's voice broke off as anger and frustration gripped him, and then recovering himself, he said, "Here, Darla, I want you to have this."

The woman, in the act of putting a part of a loaf of bread and some sliced beef into a cloth sack, paused. "What is it?"

"The money Turner had on him," he replied, passing her the handkerchief containing a roll of currency and several coins, some of them double-eagles that his brother had entrusted to his care. "Gave it to me when I saw him in the jail, along with Pa's watch and Ma's wedding ring. Those I'd like to keep."

"Of course," Darla said, staring at the money. "Won't you need some cash? It looks like there's several hundred dollars —"

"I've plenty. Another thing — I'll appreciate it if you'll keep on living here same as you have been. I don't want drifters and saloon bums taking it over. If I run into bad luck and don't come back, the place is yours."

Darla had resumed her preparations at the stove. "Thank you, Frank," she murmured, adding more items to the grub sack — coffee, a mason jar of canned peaches, other things that caught her attention. "I — I don't know how to really thank you. Turner — and you — have been so good to me."

"It's me that owes you for looking after my brother. Expect you're the best thing that ever happened to him."

"I tried to help," Darla began, and then broke off suddenly. "I almost forgot — a letter came for Turner today. I was going to take it over to the jail, but Amos Carter said —"

"A letter from who?"

"From somebody named Benbow in Fort Worth, Texas," she said, and taking a well-handled envelope from the top of the chiffonier in the bedroom, gave it to Garnett.

Benbow . . . The name sprung to life in Frank's mind. The farmer in Missouri who had sheltered Turner and him from Union soldiers who were bent on killing any and every Confederate they could find, and allowed them to stay until Turner had recovered from the wounds he had sustained and was able to travel.

"You know somebody by that name?"

Frank nodded. "Man who did Turner and me a mighty big favor once," he replied, and related the incident as he opened the envelope.

Hiram Benbow was dying in a hospital in Fort Worth, he read. The man had suffered an injury and the wound had mortified. Like as not, the physician who was writing the letter for Hiram said, Benbow would be dead by the time the letter was delivered.

"What is it?" Darla asked, noting the concern in Garnett's eyes. "What's wrong?"

"Benbow's asking us — Turner and me — to return the favor he did for us. Owns a ranch down in southeast New Mexico now, near a town called Santee's Crossing. I remember now that Turner told me the Benbows had moved away from Missouri — headed west. They wrote back and forth a few times."

Darla was tying the neck of the sack, making it as dust-proof as possible. "Now that I think of it, I remember hearing Turner mention that name before. What does he want you to do?"

"Wants us to go down to his ranch. Says his foreman, a man named Pooler, has taken over the place — sort of

71

stole it after he got hurt. He's asking us to drive this Pooler and his crowd of hardcases off the place so his daughter, Mandy, can move in and claim what's hers when he's gone. She's now living with friends in St. Louis. Don't mention his wife, so I guess she's dead."

Frank gave a moment's thought to Mandy — Amanda — Benbow. She was ten or twelve years old when he and Turner holed up on her father's farm. That would make her twenty or so now.

Darla had placed the sack of food on the table and was now beginning to fill a canteen from the water bucket. She shook her head worriedly.

"It will be too risky for you, Frank, the way things are now. The law will be looking for you everywhere."

"Can't turn my back on Benbow," Garnett said, continuing to read the letter. "Him and his family actually saved our lives. We — I — owe him."

"But you figured to get close to the border, be where you could cross over if —"

"Way it sounds, I won't be far from the Mexican border — so my chances for keeping clear of the law'll be about the same."

Frank read on. *I'm asking you to take charge of my ranch, get my debts and what I owe Pettigrew, the banker, paid off, and see to it that my girl gets started off on her own all right. Would sure suit me fine if maybe your younger brother, Frank, I recall him being named, would get together with Mandy. They'd make a fine pair. I'm hoping you're both doing good, and I sure wouldn't unload my troubles on you if I had any other way to go. So there won't be any question, I'm*

72

sending word to Ed Pettigrew that you'll be coming. Yours truly, Hiram Benbow, by J. J. Mills, M.D.

Thoughtful, Frank folded the letter, returned it to its envelope, and thrust it into the pocket of his shirt. Darla was right about the risk he would be taking, but he felt he had no choice.

Both he and Turner had made their promise to Hiram Benbow that if ever he had need of help, he had only to call upon them. The man, in his last hours on earth, had done just that.

"Everything's ready," Frank heard Darla say.

Garnett nodded. He'd best not wait any longer. Hanging the saddlebags over a shoulder and tucking the blanket roll under an arm, he reached for the sack of grub and canteen of water.

"Be obliged if you'll tell Jenny all about this in the morning. You can explain to her why I had to be in such a big hurry, and say I'll get in touch with her soon as I can."

Darla agreed. "I'll go see her first thing — maybe yet tonight."

"Might better wait. Won't be long before that U.S. marshal and Cheyenne — and maybe a posse — will be here looking for me and asking questions. They'll probably talk to Jenny, too. Thing to do is just set tight till they've made up their minds that I'm not in town."

The woman nodded her understanding. Turning down the lamp, she crossed to the door and opened it for him. She frowned.

"Your horse — I'd better help you —"

"No need — he's ready to go. I never got around to pulling off the saddle and bridle this morning, just carried in my other gear. I hang on my spurs, that'll be it."

Reaching out, Garnett took Darla's hand, pressed it reassuringly, and stepping out into the night, walked quickly to the shed where the bay was stabled.

Tying the saddlebags and roll into place behind the cantle of the hull and securing the sack of grub and canteen to the horn, he strapped on his spurs and swung up onto the bay. So far luck was with him; there had been no sign either of Cheyenne Jones and his friend working themselves free of their bonds or of some passerby discovering their plight.

Frank drew up sharply as he cut the gelding about and rode out of the yard. He'd congratulated himself too soon. A voice coming from somewhere nearby had reached him. There was a reply — cautious, restrained. Frank Garnett swore silently as he understood the conversation. His escape had been discovered and men were already out looking for him.

CHAPTER
ELEVEN

As he'd expected, the men searching for him were going first to the house — but they would learn nothing from Darla, he felt certain of that. Pulling the bay down to a quiet walk, laying a hand on the canteen to silence the faint clinking sound it was making, he moved on through the dark. He was heading south, and he realized that if he continued on that course, he would surely be seen by the posse, approaching on his left —

"He ain't going to be there," a voice, surprisingly close, cut into his thoughts. "I'm betting he's long gone."

"Dammit — he had to get his horse and gear, didn't he?" It was Cheyenne Jones. The deputy's words were angry, impatient. "Where the hell else would he've gone for them, 'cepting to that shack where him and his brother lived?"

Garnett veered the bay more to the right, angling away from the oncoming men in a westerly direction.

"Still say we ain't going to find him there. Been an hour since he busted out. He's in the saddle and running by now."

"Maybe. Just could've figured he had plenty of time. Anyway, we got to nab him before that marshal finds out his prisoner's flew the coop —"

"Expect we should've sent word to him, had him throw in with us."

"Can do that if we don't catch Garnett . . . There's the shack. Everything's quiet now."

"Hell!" A voice exploded from the waist-high brush a few yards to Garnett's left. "There he goes now!"

Instantly Frank bent low over the gelding's neck to avoid any silhouette and applied his spurs. The big horse leaped ahead, setting up a loud crackling in the dry growth as he plunged heedlessly on. Shouts went up, and among the voices Garnett could hear Jones's yelling for someone — anyone — to shoot.

Within moments the deputy and the men with him were well behind, out of the range of both voice and pistol. Frank pulled the bay down to a slow trot. The need to hurry was over — at least for a time — as the men would now have to return and get horses. That would probably require almost an hour, and in that span of time he would be well on his way south.

South . . . Garnett gave that consideration. It would be smart to change direction, lead Cheyenne and his posse — and Marshal John Crissman, who certainly would join them in the pursuit sooner or later — into thinking he had taken a different route. North was the way an outlaw running from the law would ordinarily take — north for the Dakotas and the border lying beyond.

His decision was immediate, and taking no pains to hide the bay's hoofprints, Garnett began to swerve gradually, again to the right, until he was on a direct line to the north. He maintained that course for several hours, and then when the sandy land across which he was passing became hard, rock-studded, and brushy, he cut back to his left, and making a wide circle, resumed a southerly direction.

For a time the going was slow, as he was in wild, broken country, and then he came out onto grassland, and the bay settled into a comfortable lope. By now he should be well beyond the posse's reach, Garnett figured, as the gelding had held to a good pace while moving steadily through the star-filled night. Like as not Jones and the men with him had picked up his trail somewhere in the area west of McCurdy, and now as they followed it northward while he pressed on in an opposite direction, the miles separating them would build up quickly. By morning there should be a broad strip of Kansas lying between them. He'd like to think that it would end that way, but Frank Garnett had been brushing elbows with the law much too long to believe it.

Lawmen working for a state or a territorial government would — and usually did — turn back when they reached the line between their county and the one adjacent, where their authority ceased. But it was different where a federal marshal was concerned. He or his deputy could cross over at will, and while it was considered polite and customary to notify the sheriff or similar officer of the area entered of his presence and the purpose for such, the courtesy was not always adhered to. Thus a man on the run could ordinarily rid himself of local lawmen by entering a different county, but that was not so easily accomplished if a determined federal marshal was involved.

And John Crissman, with his overwhelming hatred for any man who killed a fellow lawman, would be that kind. Frank reckoned he could count on Crissman dogging his tracks, once he got onto them, until he crossed a border — either the Mexican or the Canadian — and the old lawman would probably be waiting in the shadows for him the day he attempted to cross back.

Near first light, the bay at last began to tire, and a while later, when the pale streaks in the east showed a tinge of color, Garnett pulled to a halt in a scatter of small trees on a fairly high rise.

The gelding would need at least an hour's rest and a chance to crop at the thin grass on the hill, Frank knew — and he was feeling the need for food himself. He'd never gotten around to eating that previous evening.

Dismounting, Garnett picketed the bay on what looked to be the thickest stand of prairie grass, then sat down with the sack of grub Darla had provided. Despite the belief that he'd left the posse far behind, Frank ignored his desire for coffee, unwilling to take any chance on smoke from a fire being seen. He washed down the bites of dry bread and meat with water from his canteen instead.

He was in unfamiliar country and therefore uncertain as to exactly where he was — somewhere in

Kansas, with the Indian territory and Texas to the south and Colorado to the west, he figured. He'd have to find a town somewhere along the way to replenish his grub sack; what it held would not last long.

But mostly he needed grain for the bay gelding if he was to continue a fast and steady pace. Range grass was all right up to a certain point, but it took a daily ration of grain to keep a horse strong and able to maintain a continual run — and the lower end of New Mexico was a long way off.

In between lay more unfamiliar country, and Frank had no real idea of just what he would be up against. Water, he'd heard, was a problem in that territory, and a man was wise to keep to one of the rivers that flowed its length. It might be smart to swing deeper into Texas, a state he knew fairly well — at least its central and eastern portions. But that would take him far out of his way, and Benbow's dictated letter had possessed an urgency that gave Frank the impression that he should get to the Missourian's ranch as soon as possible.

And that's what he would do, Garnett decided as, hunger satisfied, he leaned back against one of the small trees and closed his eyes for a few minutes' sleep. If he could keep the bay moving, he'd be in southeastern New Mexico in good time, assuming —

Frank Garnett awakened abruptly. From force of habit and inner caution, he remained utterly motionless until his senses had cleared and he was fully aware of all things around him. There was no danger, he realized, and got to his feet.

Picking up his grub sack and glancing at the sun, Frank crossed to his horse. He'd slept a couple of hours, he judged, and both he and the bay were now rested. Tying the sack to the saddle horn, Garnett grasped the lower jaw of the bay and poured a small quantity of water from the canteen into the horse's mouth. That would at least satisfy the animal until they reached a spring or river — or perhaps a town where the gelding could take his fill.

Swinging up into the saddle, Garnett flung a look to his back trail. A frown creased his forehead as he saw a dark blur on the horizon. Quickly digging into one of the leather pouches buckled to the hull, he produced a brass telescope. Extending the glass, he trained it on the distant blur.

Riders! A curse slipped from Garnett's lips as they narrowed into a hard smile. He'd underestimated Cheyenne Jones. The deputy had apparently recruited a tracker, and the posse was now on his trail — a posse that was headed by not only Cheyenne but John Crissman as well.

CHAPTER
TWELVE

Garnett telescoped the glass and thrust it back into place in one of the saddlebags. It had been a watchword of his to never underestimate any man — enemy or otherwise — but he had certainly erred when it came to Cheyenne Jones.

But maybe it wasn't the deputy he should be giving credit to; undoubtedly it had been John Crissman who made the decision to bring in an expert tracker. The marshal had faced problems of like nature before, and he was now too smart to waste time on a headlong, thoughtless chase. He would first make sure he was on the right trail, and then once convinced, he'd stay on it.

Rising in his stirrups, Garnett had a long look at the country to the south and west. He wished he had a more exact idea of where he was. Could he be near the Colorado border, or was that panhandle of Indian territory known as no-man's-land closer? It was Colorado, he decided after giving it some thought, and he cut the bay gelding about, pointed him west, and spurred him into a lope.

Reaching the state line and crossing over should trim the size of the posse, Garnett reasoned, and that would be much to his liking. Cheyenne Jones was certain to turn back, and there was a good chance that the townsmen with him in the party would lose interest at that point and go with the deputy.

Such would not be true where John Crissman was concerned, however. Beside smarting over the loss of a prisoner, Crissman would be doubly determined to effect the capture, since the man he pursued was a hated lawman-killer, the worst criminal of all as far as most members of the profession were concerned.

Having a federal marshal on his trail would be a serious problem, but that meant only one man to contend with, and Frank was prepared to deal with that. With a posse of several men — riders who could separate and make it difficult for him to keep a close eye on all quarters — it was a different matter.

He had to shake Crissman — get well clear of the lawman in order to have sufficient time to fulfill the promise he and his brother had made to Hiram Benbow. How long that would take was impossible to estimate; it all depended upon the condition in which he found the Missourian's ranch and how big a job he faced in ridding the place of Pooler, the foreman, who, taking advantage of Benbow's long illness, had simply claimed the ranch for his own.

But that was a river he'd ford when he got to it. Right now his goal was to throw Crissman and the men with him off his trail and do a good job of disappearing.

Twisting about, Frank turned his attention to the north. There was no sign of the posse, nor could he see any riders to the east. He nodded in satisfaction and resumed his position on the loping bay. He was doing fine so far; if he could not see the posse, they would have no idea where he was, either.

What he needed, he realized, as he glanced about, was some kind of cover into which he could ride to shield him from the eyes of Crissman and his men when they reached a point where they could look out over the long flat he was crossing and locate him. But there was no growth of practicable size to be seen — only scattered clumps of Spanish Bayonet, thistle, and rabbitbush, with an occasional stunted juniper, none of which would be of value as a screen.

He could see the hazy blue outline of towering mountains well to the west and knew they were in Colorado, but he still had no idea if he had actually reached that state's border and crossed over from Kansas. Likely there would be a town on one side or the other, but so far he'd seen no smoke that would indicate its location.

The morning wore on. Shortly before midday, a low-hanging cloud of yellow dust well to the south drew his notice. Again making use of the glass, he saw that the cause of the rising dust was a stagecoach hurrying eastward. Again a feeling of satisfaction came to Garnett; a coach meant a road, and a road would lead to a settlement. At once Frank altered his course and assumed a long tangent designed to intersect the highway ahead without causing any loss of time or distance.

Garnett halted an hour or so after noon in a shallow swale where rainwater collected and encouraged a growth of grass. While the bay satisfied his hunger,

Frank took care of his own needs, delving into his stock of food and water sparingly since he was still at a loss as to when he would reach a settlement and be able to replenish his supply.

Once again in the saddle, and finding no indication of the posse on his trail, Garnett pressed on. Now, in the long, quiet minutes filled only with a vision of sky, rolling land, and little else, his thoughts turned to Jenny Pittman. The plans they had made for a life together had been postponed abruptly upon the death of his brother, and that thought, coupled with the fact that he'd been unable to see her to explain personally what he was up against, weighed heavily on his mind. He hoped Jenny would understand — that she would wait until he could clear his name as well as discharge his obligation to Hiram Benbow.

Jenny would, he was certain. Fair-minded and honest, she would see that both were things he must do, and thus she would stand by. But it would not be fair to have her wait too long; as soon as he could he'd write to her — and perhaps broach the idea of her joining him if he could think of a safe place for them.

Near dark, Frank came to the road on which the stagecoach had been traveling, and with a sigh of relief turned onto its well-defined course. It would be easier on the bay, which had been forced to negotiate loose sand and flinty hilltops as well as grassy areas ever since leaving McCurdy. The big horse would undoubtedly make better time.

Around full dark, with his thoughts still on Jenny Pittman, Garnett paused to scan the countryside in hopes of seeing an indication of a settlement. But there was nothing encouraging on the darkening horizon, and when the day was finally over and the clear blue overhead became a dark canopy filled with glittering stars, he pulled off the road and made camp beside a small tree.

Again he bypassed the need for coffee, unwilling to betray his location to the posse or anyone else with a fire, and made a simple meal of the bread, meat, and fruit Darla had put in the sack. A swallow or two from the canteen of water, again shared with his horse, was his only liquid refreshment.

But he was doing fine, Frank assured himself; there was every chance that he had confused Crissman and the posse when he cut southeast to gain the road, and if so, he was already beginning to get the lawman off his trail. He would like to know he was out of Kansas and in Colorado, however; that would allow him to feel that he now had only the federal marshal to be on the watch for in the days to come.

It was late the next morning when welcome proof of his whereabouts was offered him. Reaching a small stream, Garnett halted beside it to water the thirsty bay, refill his canteen, and take an hour's rest.

"Howdy —"

At the greeting, coming from behind a clump of brush on the opposite side of the creek, Frank came to quick alert. He'd hoped to avoid other travelers, and thus eliminate the possibility of their in turn encountering and being questioned by Crissman or members of the posse. Hand not far from the pistol on his hip, Garnett drew himself upright and nodded to the elderly man now considering him in a friendly fashion from beyond a leafy screen.

"Morning."

The man came forward slowly, caution evident in his actions. "Sure a mighty fine day."

"For a fact," Frank agreed, easing off slightly. From the clothing he wore, the man appeared to be a miner, and his sole weapon was an old, battered, double-barreled shotgun. "You from around here?"

The man waved indefinitely toward the high, ragged hills to the west. "Nope, there's where I belong. Been visiting kinfolk and I'm heading back home. Where you pointing for?"

Frank shrugged. "On west, mostly — once I get to Colorado."

"Colorado? Hell, you been in it since early morning, I suspect — all depending how fast you been riding."

Garnett smiled. He had the answer he'd been hoping for; Kansas was behind him — well behind him if the old man knew what he was talking about — and if matters had gone as he'd expected, the posse, with the exception of John Crissman, had turned back. And if good fortune was favoring him, the federal marshal might have discontinued his pursuit until he could advise the Colorado authorities of his presence and make known his reason for being there.

"There a town anywhere around?" Frank asked, feeling better about the chance meeting.

"Sure is — about ten miles on down the creek. That where you're heading? It's sort of south — not west."

Garnett shrugged, giving his reply careful consideration. While the old man was unlikely to run into Crissman or any other member of the posse, if there were any, he felt it best to take precautions. The miner just might mention seeing him to someone, who in turn could tell of it to Crissman.

"Like I said, I'm going west. Be more interested in one over in that direction."

The older man scrubbed at the grizzled stubble on his jaw and brushed his battered hat to the back of his head. "Well, yeh, I reckon a man could call the parson's place a town — it's on over that a'way. About a dozen folk there — and there's a store — but there ain't no saloon where a fellow can get hisself a swallow of liquor. Them people are real religious — just don't cotton to strong drink."

"I'm needing grub and some grain for my horse. Can get by without the whiskey for a few more days."

"Can find that all right at the parson's. They's another settlement, however, on to the south. Name of Hugotown. It's sort of a crossroads — can get anything you're looking for there, including a woman."

Frank nodded. "Expect it's a bit out of my way," he said, crossing to the bay and climbing into the saddle. "Take my chances with the parson's . . . Obliged to you for your time."

"You're mighty welcome," the miner said, turning back into the brush, where he apparently had left his mount. "And good luck."

"Same to you," Garnett replied, continuing on in a westward direction.

He followed that course for a half a mile and then veered back to the creek, taking the trail that ran alongside it until Hugotown — no more than a dozen structures scattered along the stream — came into view. For a time Frank considered the wisdom of waiting until dark before showing himself, weighing the importance of that against the hours lost in doing so. The latter proved to be the more important, and after locating the town's general store, he circled around behind the other buildings and entered the place by its rear door.

A young boy, somewhere in his early teens, stood behind the plank counter as Frank approached. He remained mute while Garnett made known his needs and then he sluggishly accumulated the items ordered, after which he laboriously totaled up the cost on the margin of a yellowing magazine he had been reading.

"Comes to four dollars even," he said, storing the articles in a flour sack — one different from that into which he had dumped the quantity of oats purchased.

Garnett laid a gold eagle on the rough surface of the counter and waited for his six dollars in change. When it came, he pocketed it and said casually, "Where'll I find the road to parson's?"

"You meaning the parson's place?"

"Expect so —"

The boy shrugged. "What do you want to go there for, mister? Ain't nothing but a bunch of looney old codgers that won't —"

"Didn't ask you that — asked you how to get there," Frank said sternly.

Again the boy's slight shoulders stirred. "Just go back up the creek till you come to the first crossroad — it ain't much more'n a cowpath — and follow it on west. I reckon it'll take you there."

"Obliged," Frank said, and taking up the sacks, returned to his horse.

Tying the two cloth containers together and hanging them like saddlebags over the hull, Garnett doubled back over his own trail until he was well above the settlement and completely out of its sight, and then changing course and circling wide, again rode south.

Days later a sign at the fork of two well-traveled roads advised him that he had crossed into Texas, and he realized he had entered, crossed, and departed the outlaw haven of no-man's-land, where law was nonexistent. It occurred to Frank that John Crissman, if he were still on his trail, could have swung wide to avoid that strip of land, so as not to encounter a lawless band and delay himself. If so, the marshal would be a day or two behind Frank by now.

But Frank took no satisfaction from that, fully aware that lawmen of Crissman's stripe never really gave up, and despite delays, would continue to dog the tracks of whoever they might be trailing.

He'd not make it easy for the marshal, Garnett vowed, and staying fairly near the Texas side of the New Mexico border, he kept his passage as secret as possible — showing himself only when it was necessary to purchase food.

He had no indication that Crissman or anyone else was in the area, and as time passed and the miles of empty country fell behind him and he drew closer to that part of New Mexico where he believed he would find the town of Santee's Crossing and Benbow's Ranch, he became more and more convinced that he had shaken all pursuit.

And then one bright morning as the sun beamed down from a cloudless, steel-blue sky, Frank came to a road where a sign pointing west read: SANTEE'S CROSSING — 20 MILES. Turning onto the trail at once, he rode into New Mexico.

In mid-afternoon he saw cattle off to his left and went over for a better look at their brands. A weary sigh escaped his lips as he saw the H-B that declared the steers to be the property of Hiram Benbow. He'd made it — and with no interference from U.S. deputy marshal John Crissman.

But the lawman was out there somewhere, asking his questions and doggedly pressing his search, and eventually, be it a day, a week, or a month, he'd come riding back into his life, Frank Garnett knew for certain.

What he needed now was to locate Benbow's ranch, complete the favor the Missourian had asked, and then head on into Mexico. Once he was safely across the border, he could start thinking about Jenny and their future again.

CHAPTER
THIRTEEN

More cattle came into view, but it seemed to Frank Garnett that there was little order to things. The stock was loosely scattered, not for grazing reasons — the range was in excellent condition — but as if the steers were being allowed to drift at will.

A short time later he spotted a coulee with a grove of trees and considerable brush. The bright sparkle of water proved the existence of a spring, and Frank at once veered toward it with the thought of watering the bay and treating himself to a few minutes refuge from the strong heat.

As he rode into the grove, he saw it was a watering hole for the stock. But rank growth had been allowed to accumulate in the pond and along its edges to such an extent that the cattle undoubtedly had difficulty in getting to it. Garnett was no cattleman, but he had done a few turns in the past as a working cowhand, and he recognized the signs of a ranch being neglected.

Pulling to a stop at the one break in the wall of brush, Frank swung down and moved off a few steps to allow the gelding to reach the spring. Garnett halted abruptly, anger and annoyance flooding through him. A man — a cowhand from the look of his clothing —

pistol in hand, was facing him from across the spring. A hard grin had parted his lips.

"Now what the hell you think you're going to do?" he demanded.

Frank shrugged. "Water my horse —"

"Just like that, eh? Help yourself with no howdy-do, hello, go-to-hell to nobody!"

"Didn't see anybody to ask. This is Benbow range, ain't it?"

"It sure is — and we got us a way of dealing with drifters we catch trespassing, ain't we, boys?"

Garnett heard quiet movement somewhere behind him at the words, and turned around. Two more men were closing in on him, the same hard grins splitting their mouths.

"I'll tell you now — you best back off," Garnett warned softly, hand dropping to the weapon on his hip.

"You ain't that dumb," the man holding the pistol said. "I sure ain't wanting to plug you, drifter, but if you reach for that iron again, I'll purely have to."

Frank let his hand fall away from the gun. "I've got a reason for being here," he said, facing the man with the drawn pistol. He was cornered, and admitting that fact, it was only smart to talk, to try and make the cowhands see reason and thus avoid the working over — and robbery — that he knew were in the offing for him. "And you —"

"I'll just bet my Sunday hat you do," one of the pair behind him said. "And it'll be a real jim-dandy —"

The next instant Garnett staggered forward as a blow to the back of his head sent his senses reeling. He reacted instinctively. Unsteady, struggling to stay on his feet, he came about, lashing out with a knotted fist at the nearest blurred figure. The blow connected with one of the men, brought a grunt and a string of curses from him.

"Hit the sonofabitch again!" the man holding the pistol yelled, and hurriedly waded across the spring.

Frank heard the words as if from a distance, and then as a second blow rocked him, he lashed out again. His wild swing missed, and dazed, off-balance, he went to one knee.

"Whop him again!" one of the trio shouted.

"Sure is a tough one, all right," another observed, and drove his booted foot into Garnett's middle.

Frank gasped as the shocking kick exploded breath from his lungs, and suddenly without strength, he let himself sprawl forward onto the cool, grassy ground.

"Reckon he's had enough?"

"Expect so — he ain't moving none . . . That sure is a fancy gun he's wearing. I'm going to do some swapping."

Garnett felt his .45 leave its holster, and again reacting instinctively, caught at the hand gripping the weapon.

"Hell, he's still wanting to ruckus!" Frank heard a voice shout in surprise, and felt his senses reel again as a pistol clubbed him on the side of the head.

"That'll settle him down." The words came falteringly through a wall of pain to Garnett. "Let's see what he's got on him."

He felt hands go into his pockets, reach under his shirt and around his waist seeking a money belt. From off to one side came a reply.

"Ain't nothing much in his saddlebags — a spy glass, some duds, an extra gun and shells."

"Well, I sure found something!" the cowhand searching Garnett exclaimed. "Must be three, maybe four hundred dollars in this here poke! We picked us a fat one this time, boys!"

"Where you reckon a bird like him'd get money like that?"

"Bucking the tiger, more'n likely."

"Well, can bet he sure didn't make it riding fence for some rancher."

"He ain't no cowhand — can easy see that. Duds are plenty nice and his hands ain't calloused none."

There was a laugh. "He ain't no great shakes at nothing right now. There anything else in his pockets?"

"Folding knife and some change — and a letter from somebody."

"Letter — it could maybe mean something, tell us who he is and where he's heading."

"Yeh, I guess, but I ain't no hand at reading and writing. Either one of you want to try and —"

"Naw, forget it. Prob'ly just a letter from his lady friend somewheres — one he likely was going to see."

Again there was a laugh. "He sure ain't going to be in no shape for courting now! We got his money, and Digger there's got his gun — and he's stove-in right smart."

Digger . . . Frank Garnett let the name register on his mind. His senses were still dull, but he was noting voices and storing them away in his memory as best he could. He'd not had a good look at the pair who had come at him from the rear, and it would be sheer stupidity to move or make any effort toward getting a glimpse of them — he'd taken all the punishment he cared for by that time. The incident, however, would not end there; the three cowhands might be holding the high cards now, but his turn to deal would come.

"We telling Red or Pete about this?"

The men had moved off and were now standing somewhere behind him, Garnett figured.

"Why the hell should we? I don't recollect them divvying up any of the cash they get their paws on with us. Way I'm seeing it, it's every man for hisself around here anymore."

"Yeh, I reckon you're right, Andy. We splitting up that poke now?"

"Naw, let's hold off a bit," Andy replied. "We best get away from here — somebody else might come along."

"What about the drifter? We just leaving him laying there?"

"He ain't dead, is he?"

Garnett heard a step, felt a hand press against his chest. A voice said, "Naw, he's still breathing —"

"Expect we could tie him to his saddle, spook his horse into running."

"That'd take too much time — and like I done said, somebody — one of the boys — could come along. Just leave him laying where he is. When he wakes up and figures out what happened, I'm betting he'll take off mighty fast. He ain't going to forget the lesson we learned him!"

Frank Garnett lay quietly listening to the words being spoken, taking them all in, and making mental note of what was being said. Digger, Andy, and a third man — they were the ones he'd settle with. The two others mentioned — Pete and Red — apparently were friends with whom they had some sort of a partnership.

Were they Benbow cowhands? Frank gave that thought as he heard the riders start to move off to their horses, picketed somewhere in the trees on the opposite side of the spring. It was possible; his question about whether he was on Benbow range or not had been answered in the affirmative, and there had been that remark that they had ways of dealing with trespassers — but that was not proof they worked on the ranch. They could be nothing more than outlaws, small-time holdup men who, pausing at the spring and seeing him approaching in the distance, set up their ambush. If —

The sudden, quick rush of hoofs reached Frank Garnett, and rolling onto his back, he sat up. He could not see the riders, which meant they were heading south — his view in that direction was blocked by the stand of trees and brush.

Garnett slowly pulled himself erect, simmering with hot anger and ignoring the pain and soreness the men had inflicted upon him. Hell — it didn't matter a damn which direction they took! He was going to follow and get back what was his — with interest!

CHAPTER
FOURTEEN

Coming about, Garnett moved toward his horse, anxious to mount up and be on the trail of the three men. A surge of giddiness halted him — the penalty for sudden motion. Turning, he crossed to the edge of the spring, and removing his hat, lowered his head several times into the cooling water, until finally all of the mist and cobwebs in his brain had disappeared. Regaining his feet, he retraced his steps to the bay.

Both saddlebags were unbuckled, and some of their contents lay strewn about on the ground nearby. Ignoring that bit of vandalism for the moment, Frank probed about in the leather pouches for the spare pistol that he carried. His fingers came into contact with the weapon, and removing it, he looked it over closely for any damage. One of the outlaws had taken notice of it, he recalled.

The weapon appeared to be unharmed. It was an old cartridge cap-and-ball left over from the war, and carried in its earlier days by Turner. Its action was slow, but it was better than no weapon at all, and after loading it and making it ready for use, Frank thrust it into his holster. Gathering up the clothing and other bits of personal belongings scattered around, he restored them to place in the saddlebags and stepped up into the saddle.

The three riders were not to be seen — which was what Garnett expected. They would quickly leave the area, but, flush with easy money, would do what came naturally to them and head for the nearest town, where there would be plenty of whiskey, women, and gambling available. That would be Santee's Crossing.

Frank scoured the horizon for smoke but could see none. That was understandable. At that time of day, and with the heat as it was, there'd be a minimum of fires burning. It would be smarter to find the Benbow place first, get directions to the settlement there, and then head for the town.

Reaching back into one of the leather pouches as the bay continued on at a fair lope, Garnett again removed the telescope. From a habit acquired since riding out of McCurdy, he trained the glass on the wide, rolling country behind him. For several minutes he searched carefully, and then finding nothing to cause alarm, came back around to examine the lush grazing land stretched out before him.

At first there was only the vast emptiness to behold, but gradually, well off in the hazy distance, he picked up the faint, heat-distorted outlines of several buildings. Benbow's ranch, unquestionably, he thought, and putting away the brass telescope, settled down to cover the intervening distance as quickly as possible.

An hour later Frank Garnett drew his horse to a stop at the edge of the swale in which Hiram Benbow had built his spread. It was a fine bit of ground — covered with grass, shaded by trees, and watered by a briskly flowing stream that threaded its way along the floor of the hollow.

The main house was flat-roofed and sat off to one side. Not too far from it was the cook's shack, and beyond that squat structure were several other buildings — the bunkhouse, feed and tool sheds, barn and the like. There were two or three corrals, but Frank could see no stock in them.

There were horses standing at the hitch-racks fronting both the ranch house and the elongated quarters of the crew. A dozen or more men lounged in the shade cast by the latter; there was no evidence of activity. From appearances it would seem Benbow's H-Bar-B Ranch was taking a holiday.

From this distance the place looked to be orderly and well kept, but as Frank rode nearer and approached the yard, he saw proof of neglect — buildings in need of paint, corral bars sagging or completely down, doors hanging from a single hinge, several broken windows; Hiram Benbow had failed to mention how long it had been since he left his ranch, but from its overall look at close range, Garnett judged it must have been months, for it would have taken that much time for the place to fall into its present derelict condition.

He rode past a shed or two and a wagon rusting from idleness in the glaring sun and veered the bay toward the bunkhouse and the group lazing before it. Immediately three of the party rose from the stoop where they were sitting and advanced to meet him. A flash of anger hit Garnett, who set his jaw to hard corners as he recognized the outlaws — or cowhands — who had robbed and worked him over.

"Told you plain we don't let no drifters on Benbow range!"

It was the man called Digger — the one who had confronted him at the start with a drawn pistol.

"The hell you say!" Garnett yelled as his fury boiled to the surface, and ramming spurs into the bay, sent the big gelding plunging straight at the three cowhands.

"Look out — dammit!" Digger yelled in alarm, and lurched to his left. He collided with the man standing next to him, sent him stumbling off through the churning dust to sprawl onto the ground.

The bay, fighting the bit as he struggled wildly to avoid colliding with the men, but goaded by Garnett's punishing spurs, managed to swerve slightly — but not enough. His rock-hard shoulder caught the third rider in the chest, knocking him flat.

The remaining men gathered in front of the bunkhouse had come to their feet at Garnett's sudden and unexpected onslaught. As he left the saddle in a long jump, the old cap-and-ball revolver in his hand, they hesitated as he flung a warning glance at them.

"Keep out of this!" he yelled, and pivoting, struck out at Digger with the heavy pistol.

Digger, wheeling to meet Frank, took the blow just above his left ear. The crack of metal meeting bone was loud, and Digger dropped instantly.

Garnett gave the man no notice. Anger was still roaring through him, and at once he spun, prepared to

100

meet the rush of the man accidently knocked off his feet by Digger.

"Get him, Andy!" a man on the bunkhouse porch encouraged. "Knock the bastard's head off!"

Andy came weaving in, crouched low, fists up and ready to box. Apparently he had at sometime in his life witnessed a match between professionals and fancied himself something of a fighter.

"Show him how the cow ate the cabbage!" another voice shouted.

Garnett took a long step forward. Andy hesitated uncertainly, and as Frank rocked to one side, swung a wide right. Garnett avoided the blow easily, and merciless, stepped in close and clubbed the man senseless with the pistol he was holding.

A scattered mutter of disapproval went up from in front of the crew's quarters, and from the corner of his eye, Garnett saw three men now standing on the porch of the main house.

"Come on, Irv — get in there after him —"

Onlookers were now pleading with the cowhand the bay had knocked to the ground. He had gotten to his feet, was moving unsteadily toward Garnett.

"Back off!" Frank snapped, sweat streaming down his face. "You've had enough."

Irv, a husky, heavyset man with small, dark eyes, came to a halt, staring at his friends sprawled in the dust.

"You want me to lay you down there with them, then let's get at it," Garnett continued. "Be a pleasure, seeing as how I feel after you three kicked me around."

In the silence that followed Frank's harsh words, Irv raised his hands in a sign of submission.

"Had enough," he said. "Damned horse hit me good — maybe busted my shoulder or done something to my innards."

"That's good," Frank snapped callously, and stepping up to the man called Andy, retrieved his bone-handled six-gun. Sliding it into his holster, and still holding the long-barreled cap-and-ball, he rested his cold eyes on Irv.

"Where's my poke?"

Irv pointed at Digger, now beginning to stir. "He's got it, I reckon."

"Get it — and every damn bit of it better be there!"

"It is," Irv muttered, crossing to where Digger lay. Bending down, he dug into his friend's pocket. Producing the small leather pouch, he tossed it to Garnett.

Thrusting the cap-and-ball under his belt and giving the men looking on another warning glance, Garnett checked the contents of the poke. Finding it satisfactory, he nodded crisply to Irv.

"It's all here," he said, dropping the pouch into a side pocket. "Now get your friends there on their feet and get off this ranch. If I have any more trouble with you, I'll use the bullets in my gun."

An angry mumbling came from the porch of the bunkhouse. Irv, taking courage from what appeared to be an indication of support, shook his head.

"Just who the hell you think you're talking to? It's you that sure better be getting off. I — me and Digger and Andy — we work here."

Garnett smiled coldly. He should have guessed the three men were riders working for Pooler, the foreman who had assumed ownership of Hiram Benbow's ranch.

"Not anymore you don't. Pack up your gear and —"

"What's going on here?" a voice cut in from behind Frank. "And who're you?"

CHAPTER
FIFTEEN

Frank pivoted slowly. The three men he'd noticed earlier at the main house had forsaken their places on its porch and come down into the yard. Folding his arms across his chest, he considered them.

One, in his late twenties probably, was a tall, handsome man in a dark sort of way. Beardless, he sported a neatly trimmed mustache and was dressed expensively. This would be Dave Pooler, the H-Bar-B's foreman.

The pair with him, evidently his closest friends, wore ordinary cowhand-clothing, none of which looked to have seen much service. One was a squat, husky man, the other, also of short stature, was red-haired, narrow-faced, and had the quiet way of a gunman about him.

"Name's Garnett," Frank said coolly. "You're Dave Pooler, I take it."

"You're right," Pooler snapped. "What's this all about? Just who the hell do you think you are — coming in here, mumping my boys and ordering them off the place?"

A crooked smile twisted Garnett's mouth. There was something about the dandified Pooler, other than what he had done to Hiram Benbow, that irked Frank and made what he was going to say doubly enjoyable.

"I'm the man taking over this ranch — Benbow's orders."

Pooler drew up stiffly. "Like hell you are!" he shouted as he took an impulsive step forward. He halted abruptly as Garnett's hand dropped to the pistol on his hip.

"Ain't nobody taking over this place," he added, frowning. "I'm the ramrod here, have been for —"

"You're not anymore," Frank cut in, and reaching into his shirt pocket, produced the letter he'd received from Hiram Benbow. Unfolding the sheet, he read its contents, doing so slowly and in a strong, clear voice that no one present would fail to hear and understand.

Dave Pooler was shaking his head even before Frank finished. "That's a crock of bull — and I ain't believing a damn word of it!" he said. "It's something you've trumped up —"

Garnett shrugged. "Go talk to Pettigrew, the banker. He knows about it."

The tall, one-time foreman gave that thought while he toyed with the gold watchchain and fob hanging from a pocket in his gray silk shirt. Low conversation had broken out among the men gathered in front of the bunkhouse, and Digger and Andy were now both up and on their feet, glancing about dazedly as if uncertain where they were.

"I ain't buying none of this," Pooler declared after a bit. "And you ain't driving me off. I've been doing a good job running this outfit for old Hiram near onto five years now, and nobody's just going to come in, cold turkey, and kick me out. I've done too much for that old man to let him —"

"From the looks of things, I'd say you haven't done much of anything," Frank cut in dryly. "Leastwise not for quite a spell. Cattle're all scattered, water hole I stopped at was all clogged up, and I expect others are the same. The range is overgrazed in some sections while the grass is hock-high in others.

"The house and sheds are rotting from lack of whitewash and paint, the corrals are falling down — and you've had a fire that you've not troubled yourself to do anything about. The whole place looks like a trash pile back of a saloon. Now if this is what you call doing a good job, then you best go somewhere and learn what a good job is."

"Can't get help worth a damn," Pooler said lamely.

"If Digger and that pair with him are a sample of what you hire — and you do your ramrodding setting around the house all dressed up — I can savvy why the ranch has gone to hell."

"And you're saying you can do better?"

"Any thirty-dollar-a-month cowhand could beat what you and this bunch of good-for-nothings've done!"

The redhead at Pooler's side stiffened. "You're plenty loose with your mouth —"

"When it comes to the truth," Garnett snapped. "But I'm not here to do any jawing. Pooler, I want you and your pards there off this ranch — along with any other man who sides with you."

Dave Pooler smiled. "Ain't but one of you doing all this big talking. I got maybe a dozen friends who'll back me up."

"Suits me," Frank said agreeably. "But you remember I'm dealing with you, and if it comes down to throwing lead, you'll be the first one I cut down — no matter how it comes out."

Pooler brushed at the sweat on his forehead, hooked his thumbs onto his gun belt, and glanced around. Some of the men present returned his questioning look with a reassuring nod, and others shrugged and turned away.

"You've got ten minutes to collect your gear and move on," Garnett continued. "Otherwise figure on using that gun you're wearing. It's that simple — get out or draw!"

Again the tall foreman glanced about, and then, shoulders lifting and falling in a show of indifference, he turned away.

"Can promise you one thing — you ain't heard the last of this," he muttered as he started for the main house.

Immediately the two hands who had stood beside him fell in behind. Digger, Andy, Irv, and three of the group that were on the porch of the crew's quarters also stirred themselves and followed.

Frank considered them thoughtfully, and then drawing both the bone-handled pistol and the cap-and-ball, he put his attention on the remaining men.

"I reckon you're not Pooler's bunch —"

There were several nods of assent. An elderly cowhand, angular face reddened by years in the sun, beard, mustache, and thinning hair all iron-gray, shambled forward. A happy grin split his weathered features.

"No, siree, Mister Garnett, we sure ain't!"

"Then I'm asking for a couple of you to go up to the house with me. I don't want Pooler or any of his crowd carrying off anything that's not theirs."

"Sure thing, Mister Garnett," the oldster said, motioning to the others. "We'll all be real pleased to."

"I'm obliged — and the name's Frank. You can forget the mister."

"Yes, sir — and I'm Ira Flagg. Been here since Hiram Benbow drove up from Missouri way and started up this here spread."

Garnett bobbed. "Expect you're the man I need to do a lot of talking to," he said, moving off toward the house.

He glanced over his shoulder. The entire party of cowhands, as well as what looked to be yard help, had thrown in with him and Flagg and were trailing them across the hardpack.

Frank shifted his gaze back to the house. He pointed to the extreme north end of the structure, where a broken window and the scar of flames and smoke marked the ugly results of the fire.

"How'd that happen?"

"Was Pooler and his bunch's doing — they been living in Hiram's house for quite a spell now. Just up and moved in one day."

"From the bunkhouse?"

"Yep — and we was all pleased as get-out when they done it — but they sure liked to've ruined Hiram's place. Was having themselves a big party one night. Had brought up a half a dozen gals from town — along with maybe a keg of red-eye. There was a fight. Somebody said it was betwixt Pete Dillon and —"

"Which one was Dillon?"

"That chunky-looking guy that was with Pooler — not the redhead. That's Red Hadley. They side with him all the time, like they was bodyguarding him. Makes him feel real important, I reckon."

"Anyway, there was this fight, and somebody knocked over a lamp. That there room used to be Hiram and his missus's bedroom. He'd kept it shut up ever since she died. Was a lot of clothes and papers in there, and they was them fancy lace curtains over the windows. Once the fire got started, it got bad mighty quick. Took me and all the rest of the crew to put it out."

They had reached the front of the house. Frank halted and turned to Flagg and the other men. "Like for you to just stand by, keep your eyes peeled. If you see one of them toting off something that belongs to the Benbows, speak up. I'll back you all the way."

At that moment Pooler appeared, saddlebags slung over one shoulder, several articles of clothing drapped across an arm. Dillon and the rider called Digger were close behind, each with their possessions, which looked to amount to little more than a change of pants and shirt.

"Ain't nothing so far," Flagg said as other men came out onto the porch, and then hastily amended himself. "That poncho Red's got — that ain't his, that's Hiram's."

"Hadley!" Garnett called, motioning to the man. "Leave the poncho. It's not yours."

The redhead paused, face darkening with anger. He stood for a moment staring at Garnett, and then apparently deciding to make no issue of the matter, dropped the garment to the floor and moved on.

"What about the horses they're riding? They belong to the ranch?"

Flagg gave the nearby animals, waiting at a hitch-rack, swift survey. "Reckon they're all theirs. Wouldn't catch them riding remuda stock," he said. "They're all too highfalutin for that."

Frank nodded, and arms folded, watched Pooler and his friends cross to their mounts, some throwing a hateful glance at Garnett and the men gathered around him, others indifferent and taking it all with an easy come, easy go attitude. When the last one had climbed onto his horse and was moving out, Dave Pooler, with Hadley and Dillon flanking him, swung about and faced Frank.

"Told you this ain't over yet, Garnett," he said in a voice tight with anger. "I'm aiming to settle with you —"

"Up to you," Frank replied quietly. "Can find me here anytime — now get off the property. Your time's up."

110

Pooler's features reddened, and raking his horse with spurs, he sent it lunging ahead toward the riders already pulling out of the yard, leaving Hadley and Pete Dillon to follow.

"This sure does feel good — getting rid of them," Ira Flagg said, slapping his hands together. "Now you was saying you wanted to talk — and from what we've seen, we want to listen."

Garnett grinned and jerked a thumb at the cook-shack. "Let's do our jawing over a cup of coffee," he said, then nodded to the other men. "Means all of you. If we're going to put this ranch on its feet, we'll have to pull together."

CHAPTER
SIXTEEN

"I want to make something plain first off," Frank Garnett said after he and the crew had seated themselves at the oblong table, waiting as the cook filled tin cups with coffee. "Starting now, this is a working ranch. Any man here not willing to pull his weight had best quit."

Garnett hesitated and looked around while he waited for a response. None came, but he knew men well enough to realize that it was too soon to rejoice; there would be one or two — or more — unwilling to reveal their feelings in front of friends present, who would quietly take leave later on.

"My name's Frank Garnett and I expect you to call me Frank," he continued, taking Hiram Benbow's letter from his pocket. "Want you all to hear this again, in case some of you missed it when I read it back there at the bunkhouse."

When he was finished, he returned the envelope to a pocket, and said, "You can savvy now why I'm here. Hiram Benbow done me and my brother a big favor once — saved our lives, in fact, and we gave him our promise we'd pay him back if ever he needed help. That's why he called on us — me. My

112

brother was killed a short time back, so I had to come alone. Way I see it, doing what Hiram Benbow asked me to do is going to be one hell of a big job, but I figure I can get it done if you men will stand by me —"

"Running that damned Pooler and his bunch off's the best thing that could happen to this outfit!" one of the cowhands declared vehemently.

"For certain," Ira Flagg stated. "Way things've been going around here, this ranch wouldn't've been worth doodlysquat in six more months."

"Could see things've been let slide," Garnett said. "Weren't any of you doing any range riding?"

"Was told plain by Pooler not to," a small, lean cowhand replied.

"Which I reckon was because he wanted it so's him and his bunch could do what they liked with the stock," Flagg explained.

Frank took a swallow of his coffee. "Meaning what?"

Flagg's slight shoulders stirred. "Whenever any of them was wanting money for whiskey or raising hell, they'd just round up a little jag of steers — ten, maybe twelve — and sell them off somewheres. I reckon they was scared we'd catch them doing it and do some talking."

"Did you?"

"Thought about it — but who'd we do any talking to? Pooler was running the outfit, and it'd be our word against his — and he's a right popular fellow around these parts, being so generous with his money and whiskey."

"We could sure use some money," another of the hired hands said. "We ain't drawed hardly any wages for six months. Dave kept saying we was going to make a drive, sell off some of the herd so's he could pay us — only he never did get around to doing it."

"And I'm needing vittles from the store," the cook, a hawk-faced, tall man wearing a ragged bib apron, said. "Mighty low on just about everything, but the last time I went in to Kingman's, he said he'd have to have a payment on the bill before he could credit us again. Told Pooler about it, and he said he'd square things up — but he never did."

Frank nodded. "Seems what we're needing first and real fast is money. Who was foreman here before Benbow hired Pooler?"

"Ira there," several voices replied.

"Then he's foreman again starting now, but I'll talk to you all so's you'll know what we're doing. I want about three hundred steers rounded up and drove into the corrals. I aim to sell them off quick to whoever'll pay cash. Happens I know a couple of ranchers over in Texas — not far from here — that'll maybe be interested in buying them at five dollars or so below the market. I'll send them a telegram in the morning."

"Ain't no telegram place in town," Ira Flagg said. "Have to write out what you're sending, give it to the stagecoach driver, and he carries it on to Hanson — town about fifty miles to the south. Not even as big a place as Santee's Crossing, but it's on the telegraph line."

The thought flashed through Frank Garnett's mind that since there was no telegraph office in nearby Santee's Crossing, he need not worry about any message being received by the local lawman from John Crissman concerning him. That was a load off his mind.

"Makes no difference how we do it, just so we can get off a telegram," he said. "How many steers are you running? You got any idea?"

Flagg scratched at his jaw, glanced around the table. "Ain't no way of telling how many Pooler and them've sold off, but I reckon the tally'd still run close to five thousand."

Garnett whistled softly. Benbow was well fixed for cattle. And then he realized what had happened; the ranch had been at a standstill for quite a while, with no stock roundup and no sales being made, other than the small numbers being jobbed by Pooler and his friends when they needed cash. Under such an arrangement, the herd had steadily increased, while the ranch had slipped further into debt.

"I don't know how much behind Benbow is with the bank and the stores, but we best figure on selling off at least half of the herd," Frank said finally, toying with his empty cup.

"You saying we'll make a trail drive to Dodge like we used to?" one of the riders said, his voice lifting with anticipation. "About time we was doing something like that. It's been about as exciting around here as watching paint dry."

Garnett smiled. "Guess Dodge is still the best place to deal. We'll use the cash we get from the three hundred head to pay you boys some of what you've got coming, and to square up with the general store. What we get in Dodge ought to take care of the bank and leave plenty left over for Benbow's daughter to run the ranch on."

"When's she coming?" Flagg asked.

"Don't know for sure. Benbow must have died some time ago, so I expect she'll be showing up on the stage pretty soon. That means another big job besides rounding up the cattle."

"We ain't minding work — unless maybe it's digging post holes and chopping firewood — but what are you getting at?"

"The house — it's going to need a lot of fixing up from the looks of it —"

"Place is like a hogpen," someone said. "It sure ain't fit for no woman to move into."

"Can say the same about the yard," Garnett added. "And some of the sheds and the corrals. Whole place looks like it's falling down."

"Ain't no denying that," Flagg said. "But you're talking about a lot of work getting done in a powerful hurry. That mean you ain't figuring to stay around here long?"

"I'll be here just as long as it takes to put the ranch back on its feet," Frank replied. "I — my brother and me — owe it to Benbow."

"I see," the older man said. "Now I'm wondering about something else — Pooler and his crowd. You reckon they'll leave us be so's we can get all this done?"

"They will," Garnett said flatly. "I'll take care of that."

Flagg nodded, satisfied, and then said, "And there's something else. I ain't wanting to offend you, but we're going to be needing more hands. All them things you're planning to do — rounding up cattle, fixing up the house and the place — we just ain't got near enough help to do all that."

"The hiring sign's up right now," Frank said. "If any of you knows somebody willing to work, tell them there's a job waiting here. I'll see what I can do while I'm in town tomorrow. Ought to be a few riders around looking for work."

"I expect there'll be plenty, soon as the word gets out that Dave Pooler ain't running things no more."

Garnett glanced about. "Anybody want to say anything?"

Flagg waited, and when no one spoke up, said, "Want to get this straight. Way I savvy it, first thing you got on your mind is them three hundred steers, so's you can raise some quick money."

"That's at the top of the list," Frank assured him. "Last I heard, steers were bringing seventeen bucks a head in Dodge. I figure to sell three hundred at five dollars a head cheaper — for cash. That'll give us working capital — and that's what we're needing now. Soon as you're done with that gather and have got the steers in the corrals, you can start a roundup for the drive to Dodge."

A small cheer went up from the far end of the table, and a voice said, "Sure sounds good — us cowboying again!"

"Ain't it the truth," another agreed, as they all began to push back their chairs and rise, anxious to get to work. One paused, centering his attention on Garnett.

"Frank, I know it ain't none of my business, but would you mind telling me why you stomped the hell out of old Digger and them other two — Irv and Andy?"

Garnett shrugged. "Stopped on my way in at a spring up on what I reckon's the north range to water my horse. They were there, seen me coming, and ambushed me. Was Digger that threw down on me while the others come at me from behind. Knocked me cold and took my gun and poke. I was just getting back what was mine."

"And paying them a little extra," the rider said with a wide grin. "Well, mister, it was sure a sight for sore eyes! Digger and them didn't know what'd hit them when you come a'sailing in. Expect they figured they was up against a buzz saw."

"That's what cooled off Pooler and Red Hadley. And Dillon," Flagg said. "They set themselves up as great shakes when it comes to them pistols they're packing. But you sure didn't see any of them doing any reaching after they got a squint at what was going on . . . But don't go selling them short!" he added. "I was you, I'd sure never turn my back on any of that bunch."

118

"I don't aim to —"

"That's being smart — now where you aim to throw your gear? Ain't sure the main house'd suit you the way it —"

"I'll bunk with you boys," Garnett said. "Main house is for the boss — and that's Benbow's daughter, Amanda."

CHAPTER
SEVENTEEN

Shortly after mid-morning Frank Garnett and Ira Flagg, anxious to get matters squared away with the merchants and the banker in Santee's Crossing, turned into the settlement.

"Best I see Pettigrew first," Frank said, letting his eyes run over the irregular structures that lined the narrow, dusty lane.

Like a hundred other frontier towns he'd ridden through in his time, it seemed to turn a bleak, unfriendly face to strangers, as if wanting only to serve the needs of those who lived either there or close by.

Flagg nodded and guided his horse toward a squat, flat-roofed building near the center of the settlement. Pulling up to the hitch-rack, the two men dismounted and stepped up onto the board landing that fronted the structure. Hesitating, hand on the china knob of the screen door, Garnett threw his glance along the street.

"Over there — on the porch of the Red Bull," Ira Flagg murmured in a warning tone.

Frank gave his attention to the saloon. The three men he'd had trouble with — Irv, Digger, and Andy — were lined up along the wall of the building, watching him narrowly. At that moment Red Hadley emerged, and folding his arms across his thick chest, took a place with the others.

"I reckon I'll just keep a eye on your backside while we're around here," Flagg continued.

Garnett's shoulders stirred indifferently. "If they want trouble, they can have it," he said.

Letting his gaze drift on beyond the Red Bull Saloon, a two-story affair that looked to be the largest in town and boasted not only liquor but gambling, dancing, and the fairest women west of the Missouri, Frank caught sight of a local lawman, a lean, stooped man with a pointed gray beard and trailing mustache who was considering him from the doorway of the jail.

Frank returned the questioning stare with a nod, wondering if by some remote chance the lawman had received word from John Crissman to be on the lookout for him. And then, as he had done earlier, he dismissed the possibility as unlikely; with no telegraph connection and given the irregularity of mail service, there hadn't been time enough for the U.S. marshal to notify such distant points.

Touching the men on the porch of the Red Bull again with his gaze, Garnett opened the door and stepped into the bank. With Flagg at his heels, he crossed to where an elderly man, clean shaven, hair neatly parted, and wearing a dark business suit complete with white shirt, high collar, and bow tie, was seated at a roll-top desk. Except for the teller, waiting behind the grilled window of the single cage, there was no one else around.

"Pettigrew?" Frank said, stepping up to the desk and extending his hand. "Name's Garnett. I reckon you've heard of me from Hiram Benbow."

The banker dropped the papers he was thumbing through and came to his feet at once.

"That I have," he said heartily, and smiling, added, "Heard about you from another source, too. Can't tell you how good it made me feel to hear what you did to that gang."

"Driving them off was easier'n I figured," Garnett said. "I wanted to drop by and let you know that I aim to straighten things out at Benbow's as fast as I can."

"Can only hope so," Pettigrew said. "Hiram had a fine place out there and was doing right well. Was a shame to see it go down."

"We're selling off some stock soon as we can get the cattle rounded up and make arrangements. Expect to be able to pay off whatever Benbow owes you when that's done. I'll deposit the money — you can take what you got coming and keep the rest in an account for Benbow's daughter."

"You hear when she'll arrive?"

"No, can only go by what's in the letter Benbow had that doctor write to me and my brother."

"He with you? I'd like to meet —"

"Turner's dead. Was killed a time back," Garnett said. "Guess we can look for Amanda Benbow most any time. We're fixing the place up so's it'll be fit to live in when she gets here. I'm aiming to suggest she keep Flagg on as her foreman."

Pettigrew nodded slowly. "You're not staying?"

"I figure to pull out soon as things are squared away. Personal business."

Frank Garnett grinned wryly at the two words. Dodging a federal marshal who was determined to see him hang for murder while trying to keep his promise to the woman he wanted to marry — he guessed that could be considered personal business.

"I understand," Pettigrew said, obviously disappointed. "I'm sure Ira will do a fine job once the ranch is back on the right track. Will you be needing any money until the drive's over?"

"We can get by. I'm planning to sell off a few steers quickly at a low price to raise some cash."

"Good thinking," the banker said approvingly.

"Should get enough to pay a little on all of Benbow's debts and keep his creditors happy till we get back from Dodge. We can settle up in full then."

"Well, I'd like for you to know the ranch's credit is good with me again — if you need any cash. Luck."

"Obliged," Frank said, and shaking the banker's extended hand once more, returned with Flagg to the street.

Hadley and the other three men were still on the porch of the Red Bull, Garnett noted. The town lawman, however, was no longer at the doorway of his office. There appeared to be more people along the street and on the landings of the various stores than before.

That was not to Garnett's liking. Under the circumstances, he would just as soon keep his presence in the area as much a secret as possible. A report of his activities might be innocently carried northward and come to John Crissman's notice. And figuring the time a cattle drive to Dodge City would involve, it looked as if he would be tied down to the Benbow ranch for several weeks, which wasn't a comforting thought. Abruptly Frank turned to Flagg.

"Ira, how much of a ride is it to the Mexican border?"

The older man's shaggy brows lifted in surprise. "Mexico? Now why the hell would —"

"How long?" Garnett pressed.

"Man can make it, riding steady, in a day. Why? You figuring to go down there?"

"Maybe sometime," Frank replied. "Now I want to have a talk with whoever owns the general store —"

"That'd be Amos Kingman."

"And the hardware and lumberyard man —"

"Russ Fisher runs them both."

"Then I need to stop by the stage depot and send off a couple of telegrams. After that we can get busy hiring help, if we can find any."

"Right over there's Ed Bell's livery stable," Ira said, gesturing at a fairly large, tin-roofed structure almost directly opposite the bank. "Seeing as we're close, we can ask him if he knows of somebody looking for work."

Frank nodded, and brushing at the sweat on his face, stepped down into the loose dust and angled for the stable.

Overhead the sky was blue, unmarked by clouds, and the heat was already beginning to build, despite the early hour. Off along the border of the settlement a bell was tolling, either summoning children to school or bidding a sad farewell to a deceased citizen. A dog barked nervously from behind the livery barn, and the door of a small building standing shoulder to shoulder with three more of like facade burst open abruptly. A short, thickset man — hatless, in shirtsleeves and baggy trousers, and carrying a satchel — rushed into the open and all but ran to a nearby waiting buggy.

"Doc Gittleman," Flagg explained, noting Frank's attention to the man. "I reckon he's got hisself a hurry-up call somewheres."

They reached the barn and turned into its runway. The agreeable smell of horses, fresh hay, and leather met them head-on as they walked a short distance and entered a small office in which Bell, a middle-aged, heavily bearded individual, was intently occupied in braiding a horsehair rope. Pausing, he looked up.

"Howdy, Ira," he said, and let his glance move on to Garnett. "I reckon you're the new foreman out at Benbow's I been hearing about."

"News sure does get around fast," Flagg said before Frank could reply, and made the introductions. "We're here looking for cowhands — or just about any man wanting to work, Ed. Can you think of anyone right offhand?"

"Can use riders, drovers, and yard hands. All I'm asking is that they're willing to do a day's work," Garnett added.

Bell pursed his lips. "Was a couple of fellows by here a few days ago asking about jobs. I ain't sure they're still around, but I'll send my boy over to the Jamisons' — that's where they said they was staying. If they're still looking, I'll send them out. You're a mite shorthanded, I expect, after what happened yesterday."

"Wasn't no loss," Ira said, and spat into the tin gaboon placed in a corner of the room. "Ain't a one of that Pooler crowd that's done a lick of work since Hiram got down. Just laid around sleeping and drinking."

"They dang near run the place right into the ground for sure, I hear. You looking for trouble with Dave?"

Flagg shrugged. "I ain't certain Pooler's wanting any — he sure backed away from Frank yesterday. Well, we'll be obliged if you'll see about them two you was talking about, Ed," the older man continued, as Garnett extended his hand to the stable owner and turned to leave. "We'll take it kindly if you'll pass the word along — about us hiring on."

"I sure will," Bell replied, and resumed his tedious task of rope braiding.

Back in the bright sunlight, Frank again let his attention rest on the men gathered in front of the Red Bull. Dave Pooler and two more riders — both of whom Garnett remembered seeing at the ranch the previous day — had joined the group. The sight of Benbow's ex-foreman and his crowd of hangers-on sent anger flowing through Garnett. They made him think of vultures hanging around, silently waiting and watching, and hoping for the chance to close in at the first show of weakness on the part of their intended prey.

126

"You're a'wanting to send them telegrams," Ira Flagg said, his tone a bit anxious as he noted the change in Frank's expression from one of easy friendliness to a quiet intensity. "Place to do that's the feed store. Stage stops there. We can —"

"I'm a mite thirsty," Garnett cut in, as if not hearing. "And I reckon you could use a drink about now. Besides, a place like that Red Bull Saloon's a good place to look for men hunting jobs."

"Good place to find trouble, too," Flagg said. "Can go to one of the others — Carl Larson's got a pretty good place on down a piece."

Garnett studied Ira Flagg, faint amusement evident in his deep-set eyes. "What's wrong with the Red Bull?"

"Nothing — nothing!" the older man said hastily. "It's only that Pooler and his bunch are sure keeping a eye on us — have been ever since we hit town. Dave's even got a couple of them standing on the other side of the street a'watching us."

Frank nodded. He had noticed the two lounging against the front of a building opposite the saloon and catalogued them in his mind as possible danger.

"Saw them," he said, touching his gun. "Maybe means something, maybe not. Anyway, if it's trouble Pooler wants, I'm of a mind to get it over with now and have it done with."

CHAPTER
EIGHTEEN

A hush fell over the men gathered in front of the Red Bull Saloon as Garnett, walking slowly, hands hanging loosely at his sides, directed his steps deliberately for Pooler and the men with him. Ira Flagg, strain suddenly showing on his features and in the rigidity of his carriage, was at the tall man's shoulder.

Reaching the porch of the saloon, Garnett mounted the single step and started down its length for the swinging doors. Pooler, leaning against the front wall of the structure, watched him with hooded eyes, but Red Hadley, at Dave's side, moved forward a stride as if to block Frank's passage.

A flicker of amusement again brightened Garnett's eyes as he drew to a halt. "You in a hurry to die, Red?" he asked quietly.

Hadley remained still for a long breath, and then apparently deciding it was not the right moment for whatever he was considering, stepped back. Garnett did not continue, but features a frozen mask, dark eyes cool and hard as agate, he pivoted slowly and swept the line of men with a contemptuous look.

"I'm telling you one more time — stay clear of me, my men, and the Benbow ranch," he said in a low

128

voice. "If any of you give me trouble, I'll kill you. That's a warning — not an idle threat."

After hesitating for another few moments in silence, Frank resumed his deliberate way along the porch. Reaching the doors, he shouldered them aside and entered the saloon.

Ira Flagg, still at his shoulder, whistled softly. "Close! That was sure almighty close!"

Garnett shrugged. "I've been dealing with their kind ever since I grew up," he said, letting his gaze travel the broad, well-lighted room. About a dozen people were present.

Flagg's brow clouded. "You a lawman?"

"Not the kind you're thinking about," Frank said, and made his way through the tables and chairs to the bar that extended across a rear corner of the saloon.

Silence greeted them when they reached the counter and three men standing near its center turned away and sat down at one of the tables. Garnett considered them in wry thoughtfulness. Evidently there had been talk by Pooler, or perhaps Red Hadley, that measures would be taken to avenge the treatment they had been accorded at the Benbow ranch, and expecting such, the patrons of the Red Bull were being careful to stay clear of the line of fire.

"Whiskey," Frank said as the bartender paused questioningly before him. "Suit you?" he added, shifting his eyes to Flagg.

"Be fine," the older man replied.

The drinks came. Frank laid a silver dollar on the counter, and turning about, glass in hand, elbows hooked on the edge of the bar, faced the people on the room.

"Name's Garnett — I'm running Hiram Benbow's ranch, getting it back in shape. Flagg here — you likely know him — is the foreman from now on. We're hiring on hands. Anybody here looking for a job can find one at the H-Bar-B."

There was silence, and then a man sitting over in the area reserved for gambling laughed. "Yeh, he can if he ain't scared of getting his ass shot off!"

Frank tossed off his drink, and with the glass lowered halfway, shook his head. "You thinking about Dave Pooler and his crowd?"

"I sure am. Ain't no job around worth tangling with them."

"They'll leave you be," Garnett said. "I'll see to that."

Frank swung his attention to the left as a man sitting near the entrance of the saloon suddenly rose to his feet and went outside. One of Pooler's friends hurrying to relay what had been said, Garnett reckoned.

"Can use cowhands, yard help, drovers, handymen — anybody willing to do a day's work. Pay's the going rate."

"Way I heard it, there ain't no pay," the man at the gambling table said. "Them boys out there ain't drawed wages for six months, maybe longer —"

"We're getting paid now," Flagg said, joining the conversation. "Benbow's ranch is going to be run right from now on, so don't fret nothing about being paid."

"Maybe. I'm just a'wondering how long that'll last."

The cowhand broke off as the swinging doors opened suddenly and Hadley, followed by Pooler, Pete Dillon, and four others entered.

Garnett, eyeing them coolly, returned his empty glass to the counter, and in the tense hush that had settled abruptly over the saloon, took a slow side step away from Ira Flagg. There was a quiet stir among the others who, taking their cue from the three men who had been at the bar, sought safety from the violence that all felt was shaping up.

"It'll last long enough," Frank said, holding his narrow gaze not only on Hadley but on the rest of Pooler's party as they moved deeper into the saloon and began to settle at several tables.

Red Hadley disdained a chair. He came to a stop not far from the end of the bar, and shoulders forward, head tipped low, stared at Garnett over a space of thirty feet or so.

"Something on your mind?"

Frank Garnett's voice was low and firm as it broke the breathless quiet that had gripped the room.

"Maybe," Hadley replied. "Been told you're doing plenty of bragging. I don't cotton much to bragging."

"Habit of mine to never say something I can't back up," Garnett said. "If you'd like to try making me out a liar, this is your chance."

Hadley's mouth pulled down into a humorless grin as he glanced about at his friends. "Reckon I'll just do that," he said, and suddenly rocked to one side.

Frank Garnett saw the telltale break in the man's eyes even before the first move was made, and he knew what was coming. As Hadley drew his pistol, Garnett's was already up. A single explosion ripped the silence that filled the Red Bull, setting up a chain of rebounding echoes and adding more smoke to that already hovering just beneath the ceiling.

Hadley staggered back as the .45's heavy slug tore into his chest. A frown distorted his features, and twisting half around, he fell to the floor.

Garnett, body crouched and a coiled and ready look to him, kept his motionless, cold stare now on Dave Pooler and the rest of Red's friends. Elsewhere in the saloon the hush lingered.

"This finish it?" Frank asked after a time.

Pooler got slowly and carefully to his feet. The men with him followed. "For now," he said, and started to wheel and cross to the doorway.

"The hell with that!" Garnett snapped. "If you want to try your hand, let's get at it!"

Dave Pooler hesitated, then came back around. "You're crowding mighty hard, mister!" he warned. "Best you —"

"What's going on in here?" a voice demanded from the doorway.

Garnett did not move his head at the interruption, only his eyes. It was the lawman he'd seen earlier. At close range he appeared to be even older than he had from a distance.

"You hear me?" he repeated, moving toward Hadley's crumpled body. "What's this all about?"

"Been a shooting, Zeke," the bartender replied, finding his voice. "Red jumped this here fellow. Says his name's Garnett."

"Red was a mite too slow," Ira Flagg said, a note of satisfaction in his tone. "Everybody here seen it and know he was the one to pick the fight. Turned out he come up against the wrong man."

The star on the lawman's vest read TOWN MARSHAL. He bent over Hadley, felt for a pulse. After a moment he shook his head and straightened up.

"Dead for sure. Anybody telling it different from Ira?" he asked, glancing about and resting his attention on Pooler. "He was one of your bunch — it happen just like Shanklin and Ira claim?"

Dave Pooler shrugged. "Yeh, that's right," he said, and again started for the door. As the lawman spoke he again halted.

"Take Red with you," the marshal ordered. "Ain't nobody else going to see to his planting."

Pooler's shoulders stirred once more, and motioning to the men with him to comply with the lawman's order, he moved on.

Silent, the town's marshal watched as three of Pooler's followers stepped over to Hadley, and taking him by the shoulders and legs, carried him out of the saloon into the open. When the doors had swung shut behind them, the lawman, thumbs hooked in the pockets of his leather vest, faded old eyes filled with suspicion, turned to Frank. "Garnett? That who Shanklin said you was?"

CHAPTER
NINETEEN

Garnett, tension rising within him as he replaced the spent cartridge in his pistol, nodded slowly. The possibility that the marshal had received word from John Crissman concerning him seemed remote; it must be something else that was prompting the hostility plainly evident in the old lawman's attitude. And with time to fulfill his pledge to Hiram Benbow so critically short, Frank knew he could afford no trouble that would delay his completing the task that lay before him.

"I'm Hammer — town marshal," the lawman continued, moving forward and halting in front of Garnett. His eyes were small, sharp points. "I don't take to killings."

"Weren't his fault, Zeke," Ira Flagg protested.

"Maybe so — and maybe he was just doing some strutting, letting folks see how fast he is with that iron he's carrying," Hammer said testily, annoyed at the interruption. "I know his kind — can spot them every time."

Garnett listened to the harangue absently, as he slid his weapon back into its holster. Such talk was nothing new; he'd heard it from lawmen before, and had long since learned to let it slide off his back like rainwater coming down on a round rock.

"Sure, Marshal," he said, shrugging.

"If you got yourself a grudge or something that needs settling, by God you take it down the creek a ways! I ain't going to stand for the folks in my town getting hurt by no stray bullet! Hear?"

"I hear —"

"Ain't for certain who you are — only what you are — but I was told by Ed Pettigrew that you come here from somewheres to take over Hiram Benbow's place. That's fine, but I'd just as soon you'd stay out there — not come in to town."

"Doubt if I can do that, Marshal," Garnett said, bristling slightly. He was willing to go along with the old lawman's ideas as long as they were reasonable — but no further. "If I've got business to take care of, I'll be here."

Zeke Hammer considered Frank coldly, all the while stroking his pointed beard. The majority of lawmen, Garnett had found, were fair — albeit stern — but occasionally he had encountered one, usually in a small town, who fancied himself the lord-protector over all and reveled in exercising his authority. It was beginning to look as if Zeke Hammer was one of those.

"So that's how it's going to be," the lawman said. "Wasn't wrong when I told myself you had the look of bad trouble. All right then, Garnett, I'm warning you —"

"Save your wind, Marshal," Frank cut in, weary of the conversation. "You've already done that." Masking his irritation with a smile, he touched the brim of his flat-crowned hat, pulled away from the bar, and with Flagg shambling along in his wake, headed for the door.

Wearily, Garnett moved out onto the porch. He'd done his cause with Zeke Hammer no good with his impatience, he knew, but he had taken all of the pointless wrangling he could.

Glancing around, he saw no sign of Dave Pooler and his crowd, but a small, dark man with a thin face, quiet, colorless eyes, and wearing a checked suit, turned to meet him.

"Good to see you again, Frank."

Garnett halted, a frown knotting his forehead as he struggled to remember the man — obviously a gambler.

The stranger smiled. "Steve Vogel — Studs, you may remember me by. Was a friend of your brother's back in San Antone."

It came to Garnett at the mention of the Texas town. Extending his hand, he said, "Pleased to see you again, Studs. Meet my friend, Ira Flagg."

The gambler nodded to the older man. "Happens we've met a couple of times — I run a game here in the Red Bull. How's Turner?"

Frank said, "Dead," in a flat sort of voice, and let it drop there when Zeke Hammer came through the swinging doors, and without so much as a glance, brushed by and headed up the street in the direction of his quarters.

"Heard what the marshal had to say," Vogel remarked, gaze on the lawman. "Don't let it rile you. Zeke's got a lot of bark, but he's short on bite."

Frank smiled. "His town — I won't give him any trouble if I can avoid it, but I don't run. How long've you been around here?"

"Couple of years, more or less . . . You said Turner was dead. What got him, them damn war wounds?"

"No, was something else — I'll tell you about it first chance I get. Right now I've got to —"

"Can see you're in a hurry," Vogel broke in. "I won't keep you. But what I come out here to say is that you best keep your eyes peeled for Pooler. Heard him telling Pete Dillon that something sure had to be done about you, and damn quick."

"Expected that."

"Watching you use that pistol told me you're just as good with it as ever — better maybe — but that's not much help when you've got a half a dozen back-shooters standing off in the dark waiting for you. Cutting down Red Hadley sort of took all the wind out of Dave and them — they was counting on him, I expect, to take care of you. With him gone it'll be up to all of them to do it — specially Pooler. Sort of his aim now to prove he's all the big shucks he claims."

"Obliged to you, Studs," Frank said. "Can bet I'll be on the watch —"

"With me and all the boys out at the ranch a'helping," Flagg added.

Garnett nodded. "You can see I'm in tall grass," he said with a smile. "Now if you're ever out Benbow ranch way, drop in. Latch string'll be out."

Vogel smiled. "I'll remember that," he said, as Frank and Ira Flagg stepped down off the porch and headed for the general store.

Evidently banker Pettigrew had spread the word of Frank's arrival to take over the H-Bar-B, and Amos Kingman greeted Garnett and Flagg with a broad smile, calling them both by name as if on the best of terms.

"Want you to know I'm behind you a hundred percent in whatever you have to do to get Hiram's place back on the right track," he said.

Frank voiced his thanks and said, "I understand we've got a past-due bill here. I expect to get in some money soon — not enough, probably, to clean up the account, but it'll be a good payment. When we get in the cash from —"

"From the cattle drive you'll be making," Kingman finished. "You'll be able to take care of it all — wipe the slate clean, so to speak. That'll be fine. Meantime, I want you to know your credit's good for any supplies you need."

"Appreciate that. I'll send the cook in, have him stock up for the ranch and the drive both."

"Whatever he wants," Kingman said, no doubt convinced by Pettigrew that it would be good business to cooperate in every way possible in getting Hiram Benbow's ranch back on a paying basis.

Frank experienced the same kind of reception at the hardware store and lumberyard. The proprietor stated his willingness to be of help in any way possible, and after Garnett had explained what the needs of the ranch would be, Russ Fisher said all that was necessary was for him to send in a man with a list and it would be taken care of, the cost added to the Benbow account.

From there they went to Strickland's Feed and Seed Store. All stagecoach business — including the sending of telegrams — was done with Strickland, who moonlighted as agent for the line.

The merchant accepted the messages, waiving the deposit usually required to cover the cost of the telegrams. Such consideration was due to Ed Pettigrew at the bank, Frank knew, and was doubly grateful for the banker making it as easy as possible for him to get things underway.

Sending off the wires to Texas was the final chore that Garnett had to accomplish. Well before noon, he and Flagg headed back to the ranch.

Reaching the H-Bar-B without incident, Garnett notified the cook that their credit was once again good at Kingman's store, and advised him to not only restock the kitchen, but to lay in a supply of grub for the trail drive as well.

Relying on Flagg's judgment, Frank selected a man reputedly good at carpentry and directed him to make up a list of supplies needed for doing all necessary repairs to the house and take it to Fisher at his store. The work was to be done at once, he told the somewhat elderly yard hand chosen to handle the job.

The range crew — what there was of it — was already out rounding up the steers Frank hoped to sell immediately. Late in the day, when three men rode in in search of work and were quickly hired, Garnett began to feel much better about things.

With his mind eased, Garnett's thoughts turned to Jenny Pittman and the plans they had made and then been forced to abandon.

How fine it would have been for them if there had been no trouble with Tom January. He and Jenny could have gone ahead with their marriage, and then in compliance with Hiram Benbow's request, ridden together to the Missourian's ranch and worked at putting it back into shape for Benbow's daughter, Amanda — Mandy, as he remembered her parents had called her.

After the girl had come to take over, chances were she'd ask him to stay on, continue as the head of the H-Bar-B. Having been raised in the city, she'd have no knowledge of how a ranch should be run, and while he lacked much knowledge in actual cattle-raising, it would be he who kept things going smoothly, while depending on Ira Flagg and men like him to handle the stock.

Like as not, Jenny and Amanda would become fast friends. And who could say but that Benbow's daughter just could come to pine for city life again and offer to sell him the ranch? Garnett's pulse increased at the thought. A ranch of his own — his and Jenny's! No more riding the frontier in search of outlaws with a price on their head, while keeping an eye on the dark shadows where danger might lurk. And —

Frank, sitting on the steps to the bunkhouse enjoying a cigarette, impatiently brushed his thoughts aside. It

140

was damn foolishness to dream of what might have been; the thing a man had to do was face reality and make the best of the cards luck had dealt him.

And that's what he could do. As soon as possible, barring the arrival of John Crissman or a bullet in the back from Dave Pooler or one of his crowd, he'd send word to Jenny and ask her to join him. They'd make a life together for themselves somehow — even if it was in Mexico.

CHAPTER
TWENTY

That following morning four more men looking for work presented themselves at the ranch and were hired. By night the three hundred steers destined for quick sale had been driven in and were restlessly waiting in two of the larger corrals. Riders were busy elsewhere on the range moving stock toward the swale, where it had been agreed the herd for the drive to Dodge City would be gathered.

"Be ready to start out in maybe ten or twelve days," Ira Flagg told Garnett a week or so later. "Best we start getting things together."

Things — extra horses, more drovers, a fully stocked chuck wagon, and other necessary equipment.

"Going to take twenty, maybe twenty-five drovers," Ira said. "But I reckon you know that."

Frank, standing with his foreman at the corner of the bunk house, idly watching the yard hand who had undertaken repairs on the main house replace a broken window, shook his head.

"No, when it comes to ranching and driving a herd of steers I have to depend on you. How short are we on horses?"

"I ain't so sure we are. The way it's been around here, them that we have just got to running loose and scattered to hell. I got some of the boys popping them out of the brush and hazing them in now. Ought to know where we stand pretty soon."

"Whatever we're short, just figure on buying. I can get some cash from Pettigrew if we need it. How about the chuck wagon? It in good enough shape to make the trip to Dodge?"

Flagg nodded. "That's one thing we won't have to fret over. Hiram got a brand-new one about a year before he went down. It's only made one drive."

That information brought a smile to Garnett's lips. "Good to hear about something here that hasn't gone to hell. What about drivers?"

"I got the word out that we're hiring on for a drive. Expect some'll come drifting in — always do." The older man paused, his brow wrinkled as he stared out over the low hills to the west.

"They's something been bothering me, Frank," he continued after a time. "I just can't see Dave Pooler setting back and letting us do all this without trying to mess us up somehow. He seems to back off from doing something to the ranch, but once we get the herd moving on the trail, I ain't so sure he'll keep on holding off."

"Been thinking about that, too," Garnett said.

"Was wondering if you figured on riding with us. I could bet he'd stay clear of us then," Ira said.

"Maybe. Problem is, the drive's going to strip this place of help, and Pooler and his crowd could take that as an invitation to ride in, rustle a few steers to fatten their pokes — and they just could do a lot of damage to the place."

"Be like them, all right. They're hoping to get even," Ira agreed.

Frank Garnett also considered the personal risk to himself if he made the month-long trip to Dodge City and back. Certainly by then every lawman from the Mexican border north would have a wanted poster on him, and somewhere along the way he undoubtedly would encounter one with a sharp eye.

Frank had weighed that very real possibility and decided it was a chance he'd have to take, should it become necessary for him to take part in the drive. Getting to Dodge City as fast as possible, yet without the undue haste that would run fat off the steers, and arriving with as small a loss sustained in fording rivers, weathering thunderstorms, and battling other calamities as possible were important to the H-Bar-B, for it needed every cent that could be raised to pay off its debts.

"Expect you've made the drive to Dodge before," Frank said thoughtfully as he rolled a cigarette.

"Yeh, just about every dang year after Hiram got a herd built up and the place was going good."

"He go with you?"

Ira stroked at his chin. "Only the first time, as I recollect. After that he just left it up to me — until he took on Dave Pooler and made him the boss."

"Been wondering about that. Why would Benbow hire a no-account like him?"

144

"Was a puzzlement to me, too. I always figured it was because of the little gal — she was maybe fifteen or sixteen at the time. She took a shine to Dave, and anything she wanted Hiram seen that she got right quick. Was to please her, I'd say, that Pooler was hired on."

Frank puffed on his smoke absently. "I hadn't heard they were acquainted. Pooler play up to her any?"

"Nope, I can say that for Dave. He didn't let it get nowheres. Course she weren't nothing but a kid then, and he was putting in his spare time with the growed women at the Red Bull and such. She finally got fed up with living on a ranch — and maybe the way he was treating her — anyway, she went back to Missouri to live with her ma's folks. I seen a couple of letters come from her to him after she left — could've been more, for all I know, because she had it pretty bad for him."

"Dave write her back?"

"Wouldn't know. I reckon he could've."

Garnett said, "I see," and drew to attention as two of the ranch hands, a rider crowded between them, trotted into the yard.

"Now what —" Flagg began, frowning as he also came to the alert. "Why, that's Digger that Tex and Swede's got collared!"

The two members of the crew shepherded Pooler's man up to them, whereupon the taller one pulled off his high-crowned hat and sleeved away the sweat on his forehead.

"Me and Swede spied this jasper a'hiding in the brush, having hisself a look-see at the steers in the gather. We figured he was up to no good, so we snuck in and dropped a loop over him and brought him along."

Frank crossed to Digger, who sat head down, shoulders sagging, in his saddle.

"You looking to catch a bullet?"

Digger stirred, shook his head. "Hell, I wasn't doing nothing —"

"Trespassing on Benbow range — that's what you was doing!" Ira Flagg snapped. "You was told plain to stay off."

Garnett grasped the headstall of the horse. "Dave send you out here to see what was going on?"

Digger made no reply. Tex, leaning forward, gave the rope he held a hard jerk.

"Maybe if I was to put him on the ground and do a bit of dragging through that patch of prickly pear over back of the barn, his tongue'd loosen up a mite," he suggested.

Instantly Digger found his voice. "Dave was just a'wondering how things was coming — what you all was up to. Somebody said you was figuring on a drive —"

"You heard it right," Garnett broke in harshly. "And I want you to tell Pooler that if he gives any of the drovers trouble — him, you, or any of the rest of your bunch — I'll be looking to square up."

"You bossing the drive?" Digger asked in an offhand way.

"Now, that ain't none of your damn business what he —" Flagg shot back angrily, but Frank silenced him.

"Expect I will, so if Pooler wants to find me he knows where I'll be . . . Turn him loose, boys — and if you ever catch him or any of the Pooler crowd on our range again, don't bother to lasso them, just start shooting."

"Yes, sir!" Tex said, and shaking his rope free, slapped Digger's horse smartly across its hindquarters and sent it lunging forward. "Skedaddle, dang you, or I just might use my shooting iron right now!"

Digger, sawing on the reins, got his mount straightened out and thundered out of the yard, leaving the grinning Tex and Swede to follow at a leisurely pace.

"Expect that gives us the answer we were looking for," Garnett said as the dust settled. "I'll turn the drive over to you and stick around here."

"Best thing," Flagg agreed. "Dave's aiming to pull something, and if he thinks you're gone, he'll make his try soon as the herd's out of sight. Means we maybe better hire on three or four extra men — use them as outriders. That'll let the drivers stay with the herd if trouble shows up. Didn't figure we'd need to do that if you was coming along."

Garnett made no response, his attention again on the gate through which a rider was entering the yard.

"That's Benny — Strickland's boy," Ira said, noting the new arrival.

"Probably an answer to one of the telegrams I sent — or maybe to both," Garnett said as he moved toward the boy, who had halted nearby and was looking around uncertainly.

"I'm Frank Garnett. You got a telegram for me?"

"Sure have," the boy replied, and handing a folded paper to Frank, wheeled his horse about and headed back for town.

Unfolding the sheet, Garnett glanced at the words scrawled across it. Smiling, he looked at Flagg.

"Guess we're in business. We've sold those three hundred steers for twelve dollars a head — cash money."

CHAPTER
TWENTY-ONE

During the subsequent week, the Texas rancher presented himself with a draft for thirty-six-hundred dollars and claimed the stock he'd purchased. Four more men came looking for work, just as Flagg had prophesied, and were hired. A fifth, said by Ira to be a friend to Dave Pooler, was turned away.

The repairs on the ranch house and the various other buildings, as well as the overall cleaning up of the place, were all but finished. The herd had been gathered and the drive to Dodge City was almost ready to get underway.

"How many more riders'll you be needing?" Garnett asked Ira Flagg early that evening.

He had been to town earlier, cashed the draft, paid substantial amounts on the ranch's debts at Kingman's and Fisher's, and now, with supper over, was settling back wages with the hired help.

"Could sure use six or eight — figuring on outriders, like I said," Ira replied. "Except I can pick up a couple or so on the trail — always do, though that can be risky. Some of them riders are real cute — join up with a man, then cut his throat first chance they get."

Frank nodded. "Happens oftener than you think. I sure would like to be coming along, but I've got a hunch I'd best stay here."

"For sure," Flagg said. "Who'll you be keeping with you?"

"The three fellows you said weren't in fit shape for trail driving — Cully Smith, Rudy Schreiber, and Ollie Farwell."

"Yeh, they're all busted up some. Most places would've let them go a long time ago, but Hiram didn't cotton to that. Heard him tell them once they had a job here long as they wanted."

"They can still set a saddle and shoot, and that maybe is what I'll be needing."

"You and three men — that's stretching it pretty thin for looking after the stock we got left and the ranch, too. Reckon you can manage?"

"I'll manage," Garnett said.

The last man had been paid off, and the money Ira Flagg figured he would need for expenses on the drive had been placed in his hands. There was still a surplus — small, but ample to carry on with until Flagg returned with the draft for the sale of the herd.

"No need telling you how important it is for you to get back safe with that check," Frank said, glance now on the last of the crew leaving for town to celebrate with their earnings.

"Don't fret none about that. I'll get back — and with every dang dollar we'll be getting for them steers! I'll have enough cash left by the time we get to Dodge to keep the drovers happy — and get them home. Now, if you want to pay them a little bonus for the good job I'll be asking them to do, you can when you see us riding back into this here yard."

"They'll get it — and you can tell them so," Garnett said. "What time you moving out in the morning?"

"First light," Flagg said. "We're all set."

The H-Bar-B foreman was as good as his word. Frank watched Flagg and his drivers move the herd out shortly after the sky to the east filled with pearl, all amid a great deal of shouting and cursing. A quarter-hour or so later, the cook in his well-loaded chuck wagon and the wrangler with the remuda followed, taking the same northerly course.

Frank returned then to the ranch and had a self-prepared breakfast with Ollie Farwell, who had also done kitchen duty for himself. Smith and Schreiber were on the range, keeping as good a watch as possible over the remainder of the herd.

"Got to go into town," Garnett said when the meal was over. "Don't like keeping all this extra money on the place — and I'd sure like to scare up a cook."

Farwell rubbed at the stubble on his jaw. "How you going to keep Pooler and them from knowing you didn't go on the drive? You show up in —"

"Chance I'll have to take — but I expect they already know better. Most of the crew went to the Red Bull last night to blow their wages. Word was bound to've slipped out."

"Yeh, most likely. You stay off the road, circle by the buttes east of town, you can maybe keep from getting spotted riding in."

"Aim to go by the bank, and then see Ed Bell at the livery stable —"

"You follow that trail around the buttes, it'll take you into the bank from its hind side. Ain't hardly nobody will see you if you go that way."

Garnett nodded. "What I'll do. Won't be gone long, and while I am, want you to stick close — right here in the yard."

"Sure. What about Rudy and Smith? They'll be showing up to eat — they been out on the range all night. You want them to go back?"

"No, they're to stay here with you —"

"But what about the stock? Won't be nobody riding herd —"

"Nothing we can do about that — leastwise not right away. I figure the ranch is in more danger than the herd, so we best stand watch over it."

Farwell pushed back his chair and walked heavily to the door, his heels making a loud, hollow sound. Pausing at the exit, he glanced back.

"Sure do hope you can find that cook," he said, and then added, "I'm getting my rifle and doing some setting on the porch of the house where I can see right good. That be all right with you?"

"Fine," Garnett said, downing the last of his coffee. Rising, he crossed to where the elderly cowhand stood. "Just don't be bashful about shooting if somebody shows up that doesn't belong here."

Ollie Farwell cocked his head to one side and grinned. "Being bashful ain't something I've ever been accused of," he replied, and continued on into the yard.

152

Frank nodded and said, "Glad to hear that," moving on to one of the corrals, where he had tied his horse. Mounting, he started for Santee's Crossing, following the roundabout route suggested by Farwell. He saw no one during the ride, and when he drew up behind Pettigrew's bank building and entered by the side door, he felt certain no one had seen him.

The banker welcomed him with a broad smile and extended hand. "Pleasure to see you, Garnett. From what I'm told, things are coming along fine out at Benbow's. Even heard this morning that your cattle drive got underway."

"And I'm supposed to be with it," Frank said. "I'll ask you not to mention that you've seen me — goes for him, too," he added, jerking a thumb at the teller.

Pettigrew frowned. "Of course — but why're you keeping it a secret? Expecting trouble?"

"Knowing Pooler's kind, I'm pretty sure he'll try something . . . Got the cash left from the sale of those steers. Like to deposit it in Benbow's account — didn't want it laying around the place."

The banker took the currency and coins Frank had tucked into a small sack. Handing the muslin bag to the teller, he directed that a receipt be written out, and then once again faced Garnett.

"What about Dave Pooler? You really think he'll try getting back at you in some way?"

"I look for it — always figured being on the safe side is best. Tried to make him believe I went along on the drive, but I'm not sure it worked. We — Flagg and me — thought that'd keep him away from the drive, and whatever devilment he had cooked up he'd center on the ranch — and I'd be there to take care of him."

A knowing smile pulled at the banker's lips. "Sort of sucking him in to making a move and then trapping him, that it?"

Frank shrugged. "Can call it whatever you please. I just don't aim to let him and his bunch tear down what we've managed to build up."

"I don't blame you," Pettigrew said quickly. "I got a letter from Amanda Benbow yesterday. She'll be arriving in a few days."

Garnett swore softly. "I'm not ready for her yet. Still some work to do on the house — had to pull the men off that were doing it, send them with Flagg. Left me with only three hands — and I need them to watch the herd and the house. You have any idea just when she'll get here?"

Pettigrew shook his head. "In a few days — that's all I can tell you. There's no way you can put her up yet?"

Garnett drew out the makings and began to roll a cigarette. "Depends on her. If she's real hoity-toity like Flagg seems to think, she'd not be satisfied with the house the way it is . . . I wish to hell she'd waited a month or so."

"You could have her stay at the hotel —"

Frank struck a match to his smoke, sucked it into life. "That'll have to be the answer. I'll try to rustle up some more help —"

"Ed Bell sent a man out to see you this morning. Didn't you run into him on the road?"

"No, I came by the buttes, hoping not to be spotted by Pooler or one of his crowd. Sure glad to hear about it. Can use a half a dozen more, if Ed asks."

"Something else I think you ought to know — a letter came for Pooler from Amanda, too."

Garnett puffed on his cigarette as he silently considered that bit of information. He said, "I guess she still thinks he's the foreman."

"Could be, but I'm inclined to believe it's more than that. The girl was plenty sweet on him when she was living here with her pa. Could be she's never got over it."

"Was young then, according to Flagg."

"Wouldn't make any difference, I don't think."

Frank sighed. "That's all I need — a moonstruck girl on my hands who's got a hankering for a crooked jasper like Dave Pooler!" he said, and picking up the receipt for the money deposited, turned for the side door.

Again avoiding the street, Frank hurried back to the ranch. He had some fears concerning the welcome Ollie Farwell might have given the man Ed Bell had sent out, but as he rode into the yard he caught sight of a stranger sitting on the porch of the ranch house with Farwell, and guessed all had gone well.

The new man, Charlie Skinner by name, agreed to sign on as combination cook and yard sentry, and was immediately put to work preparing for the next meal. There had been no other visitors, Farwell said. But Frank took small comfort from that. Likely he was expecting Pooler to make a move too soon — the day was only half over.

Also, although he had made no special effort to look for Dave and his men in town since he was reluctant to let himself be seen, there had been no sign of them. Could it be that they had set out to follow Ira Flagg and the herd? It was a possibility — but Ira had assured him that neither Pooler nor anyone else bent upon a raid would catch him napping.

Garnett decided he had no choice but to accept the older man's advice — he could not be in two places at once. What he'd best do was figure out how he, with only four men, could protect a herd of a few thousand steers as well as the ranch itself, should it become necessary. And Frank Garnett was certain that it would.

CHAPTER
TWENTY-TWO

"We'll switch off watching the herd and the house," Garnett said that evening when he and the crew had gathered in front of the bunkhouse. "Have to work together. If any of you gets sleepy, let your partner know, then take a catnap."

"You figure Pooler and his bunch'll hit us for sure tonight?" Cully Smith asked.

"Nothing's for sure, but there's a good chance, and take nothing for granted. I want three men with the herd riding back and forth. Cattle're all bunched in that hollow where there's a spring, so you won't have to cover much ground."

"Charlie and me'll take care of things here. Tomorrow night we'll trade off. The signal if there's trouble will be two quick shots. Any of you hear it, head for where the sound came from fast."

"You reckon it'll be smart to go off and leave the ranch if somebody starts something? Could be a trick."

"Thought of that," Frank said. "Whoever's on watch here — one of you stay put. Means tonight, if Pooler's bunch try to rustle any steers and you men need help, I'll come; Charlie'll look after things here . . . All clear?"

The men nodded, and the three drawing range duty turned to their horses, mounted up, and rode off into the growing darkness.

Garnett nodded to the cook. "Expect we'd best split up. Take the house if you like — can see most of the yard from the front porch. I'll climb into that wagon down by the corrals. From it I can see just about everything else."

Settling down in the vehicle, which was used for hauling supplies from town as well as general yard work, Frank made himself as comfortable as possible in its splintery bed. As the hours of the warm, soft night, glowing with starlight, wore on, his thoughts drifted again to Jenny Pittman and their future. Was it right to ask her to share the life of exile with which he was faced? Mexico — he'd heard it was not the best place for a woman, unless she was a member of some wealthy family.

Living was hard, they said — and it would be doubly so for a wife whose man was on the run, not so much from the law north of the border, but from bounty hunters.

It was a strange feeling — an odd twist of fate; he himself was a man who searched for and captured wanted criminals for the reward it would bring, but who now found the situation reversed. He was the hunted, not the hunter — an outlaw forever unless he could someday force the truth out of Cheyenne Jones.

Thinking of Jones set Frank to wondering about John Crissman. Was the federal marshal still combing the country to the north where he'd lost the trail, or had he returned to McCurdy to set about issuing wanted posters to all lawmen, warning them to be on the lookout for him? The latter was more likely; a federal marshal with years of experience behind him recognized the futility of searching a land as vast as the western frontier in a haphazard manner, and was more inclined to utilize the efforts of other lawmen — alerting them to the identity of the man being sought, and then sitting back to await results.

If that was the way of it, and Frank was certain it was, his days on the H-Bar-B ranch were numbered. Marshal Zeke Hammer, already having made it clear he was no friend, would eventually get his copy of the poster, complete with Frank's likeness, and be coming to make an arrest.

Garnett scrubbed at his jaw uneasily. He could only hope that that moment was well off in the future. It would be at least a month before Ira Flagg returned from Dodge City with the money for the sale of the herd, and while it appeared that Amanda Benbow would soon arrive to take over her father's ranch, Frank had hoped to stay around until she was firmly established and Flagg was on hand to shoulder full responsibility as foreman.

Just what would he do if Hammer came for him? Garnett gave that consideration while listening idly to coyotes yipping noisily in the distance. He'd not use his gun on the old man, that was certain. The law was something to be respected if the man representing it was sincere and honest — and as far as he could tell, that applied to Zeke Hammer.

He'd simply be forced to ride out, make a run for Mexico. It would trouble him to know that he had not completely fulfilled his pledge to Hiram Benbow, but if the Missourian were around he'd understand. He had rid the ranch of Dave Pooler and his thieving crowd, had seen to its being cleaned up, repaired, and put it on a successfully running basis — and there would be plenty of money in the bank at Benbow's daughter's disposal.

Even if he had to leave before Flagg got back, the girl would be all right. He'd ask Pettigrew at the bank to look out for her, and the same could be expected from the merchants in the settlement and Zeke Hammer. Things should hold together until Flagg returned and took charge; after that Amanda Benbow would have no problem.

Garnett, tiring of his position in the wagon, climbed down. Making a leisurely circuit of the yard and finding nothing to arouse alarm, he crossed to the house. Charlie Skinner was dozing in a chair on the porch, but he came awake instantly at the grate of Garnett's boot heels in the sandy soil.

"Something wrong?" he asked, coming to his feet.

Frank shook his head. "So far, nothing," he replied, and moved on back toward the wagon, listening idly as before to the coyotes filling the warm, hushed night with their discordant barking.

Near dawn, when an early chill began to set in, Charlie stirred himself and went to the cook's shack to brew a pot of coffee. When it was ready, he reappeared with a cup of the steaming black liquid in each hand and moved to where Garnett had stationed himself.

"A little something to open your eyes," he said, passing one of the tin containers to Frank.

Garnett, again dropping down from the vehicle, accepted the coffee gratefully with a nod. "Can use it," he said, and took a swallow.

"A drop or two of whiskey maybe'd help, but there weren't none around," Charlie said, half apologetically. "I reckon the boys out there on the range got through the night. I didn't hear no shooting."

"Just what I hope that means —"

Charlie took a swig from his cup, brushed at the moisture left on his mustache. "You reckon we could be doing all this for nothing?"

"I'd like to think so, but from what I've seen of Pooler and that bunch that runs with him, I doubt we can be that lucky," Garnett said, and shifted his attention to the gate. He drew up sharply, a frown furrowing his forehead. "It's Cully and Rudy Schreiber. Something's wrong."

"One of them's hurt," Skinner said. "It's Rudy."

Frank set his empty cup on the wagon and hurried forward to meet the two men. Smith, seeing him, veered toward them.

"Rustlers — was about a dozen steers run off, Rudy told me," Cully said, his voice taut with anger. "I found him beat up something fierce, laying in the brush."

Garnett had lifted the dazed and suffering Schreiber from his saddle and was carrying him into the bunkhouse. He stiffened as he got a closer look at the elderly cowhand. Rudy had taken a terrible beating about the head. Laying him out on his bunk, Frank wheeled to Cully.

"Did he get a look at who worked him over?"

Smith nodded. "Said it was Digger and Irv and another one of Dave Pooler's bunch — didn't know his name. He caught them driving off the steers, but before he could signal for help they jumped him."

Garnett was already turning to the door. "I'm going to town after Pooler — aim to stop this kind of business right now. Do what you can for Rudy — I'll send the doc back soon as I get there."

CHAPTER
TWENTY-THREE

Santee's Crossing was up and about its daily routine when Frank Garnett rode in. He went directly to the office of the town's physician and found him dozing in a chair behind his desk. Evidently he had just returned from an early call.

"I'm from the Benbow place," Frank said, rousing him. "Got a man out there that's bad hurt."

The doctor came immediately to his feet. As he reached for his bag and hat, he said, "What's wrong — what happened to him?"

"Took a pistol whipping —"

The physician considered Garnett's set, grim features briefly. "It seems you know who did it —"

"I do," Frank replied as they moved out into the open. "Going there now . . . Do what you can for Rudy, Doc."

"Naturally," the physician said, and hurried to the horse tied to a tree at the rear of his quarters.

Frank crossed to the rack where he'd left his bay. Jerking loose the slipknot in the reins, he swung up into the saddle, cut the gelding about, and pointed for the Red Bull Saloon. It was early, and he doubted he'd find Dave Pooler and his crowd on hand, but they — Digger and Irv — might be around, and the anger that was throbbing within him would not permit him to remain idle. If they were not there, possibly someone could tell him where they might be found. Since they no longer lived at the H-Bar-B, they would have to be slinging their gear somewhere in the settlement.

Reaching the saloon, Frank drew his horse to a stop, and securing him at the long rail fronting the place, stepped up onto the porch and shouldered his way through the swinging doors. A glow of satisfaction filled him. Pooler was there, standing at the bar with a drink in his hand. Alongside him were Pete Dillon and three other men — but there was no sign of Irv or Digger.

Pooler glanced around as Garnett entered the otherwise deserted room. A sneer curled his lips. "Well, looky here, gents, we got company!"

Cool, Frank continued to advance further into the saloon, until he reached the end of the counter. The bartender studied his grim features anxiously.

"I'd sure be obliged if you'd —" he began in a tentative voice, but hushed as Garnett waved him off.

The expression on Pooler's face changed, and a wariness came into his dark eyes. "You got something sticking in your craw, mister?"

Frank remained silent as tension claimed the saloon, all the while narrowly watching Dillon, who took a slow step to one side, away from Pooler, as if making room for himself. He halted under Garnett's hard stare.

"You know why I'm here," Frank said evenly. "You had your boys beat up one of my cowhands last night and drive off a dozen H-Bar-B steers."

164

Pooler shook his head. "You're loco — I don't know nothing about it."

"Don't lie to me! Man they jumped recognized two of them — Digger and Irv."

"Digger and Irv," Dave repeated. "Hell, I ain't seen them since supper last night."

"They're working for you — if you can call rustling and stealing work — and I aim to settle with them for what they did to Rudy. Meantime, I want those steers drove back onto Benbow range."

Pooler finished his drink, set the glass on the counter, and glanced at Dillon and the other men with him. "Any of you know what he's talking about?"

The gunman shook his head, as did the riders with him. Garnett smiled crookedly.

"You think I'll swallow that? Not even if you swore on your mother's grave! Now, damn you, start talking. I want to know where Digger and Irv and whoever else was with them can be found. Somebody better speak up!"

A silence followed Garnett's hard words. Outside in the street, the sound of iron wheels cutting into the loose dirt and the thud of hooves announced the arrival of the stagecoach, while from the leafy cover of a cottonwood behind the saloon a desert thrasher sent his song into the saloon through an open window.

Pooler signaled for another drink. "Damnit all, Garnett, I'm telling you straight! I don't know nothing about it. You think I'd be looney enough to rustle H-Bar-B cows now? Hell, I ain't about to foul my own nest!"

"What's that mean?" Frank asked after a few moments, during which he puzzled over the man's words.

"Mean?" Pooler replied, grinning as he took up his drink and glanced about at his friends. "Means I'll be taking over and running Benbow's ranch again."

Garnett's jaw tightened. Evidently the letter Dave had received from Amanda had led him to dream of greater things.

"Not hardly, Pooler — not while I'm around —"

Dave shrugged. "I can maybe fix it so's you won't be."

"You're welcome to try — anytime," Frank said. "Best I remind you, however, that your other attempts didn't work out so good. Doubt if another try will come out any better . . . Now I want those steers back on H-Bar-B range by sundown — and you tell Irv and Digger I'm looking for them."

Pooler stirred indifferently. "Sure — if I see them."

Garnett's smile was as cold and dry as a winter wind. "Take my advice — see them," he said, and pivoting on his heel, returned to the street.

At once the Strickland boy came hurrying up from the stagecoach, which was halted now at the make-shift depot. "Got a letter for you," he said, handing over an envelope. "It just come in on the southbound."

Garnett murmured his thanks, and with a deep frown creasing his brow, ripped open the envelope. He glanced first at the signature penned at the bottom of the sheet. Apprehension filled him. It was from Jenny.

166

Dear Frank, it began, and then continued in her small, precise handwriting: *I have to warn you. Marshal Crissman and Deputy Jones somehow forced Darla to talk yesterday, and made her tell them where you had gone. She killed herself this morning when she realized what she had done.*

Crissman started south today. He said he wouldn't be back until he had you in chains. I'm getting this letter right off, in hopes it will get to you before he does.

Frank, I've waited long enough. Let me know where you'll be, and I'll meet you there as soon as I can catch a stage. Please answer right away. Love, Jenny.

Garnett thoughtfully folded the sheet, returned it to its envelope, and tucked it into a pocket. He had figured it would be Zeke Hammer who finally came for him, not John Crissman. He guessed the fact that Crissman was coming for him personally was a good indication of how much hatred the lawman bore for him.

Moving to his horse, Frank took up the reins and mounted, his eyes unconsciously going to the jail as a renewed wariness possessed him. Hammer was not in sight — nor was there any sign of Crissman. It was too soon for him to be there, Garnett assured himself. A stagecoach running fast and changing teams at regular intervals covered distances with greater speed than a man on horseback. Odds were good that he'd have at least a couple of days before the federal marshal arrived.

His thoughts came back to the letter — to what Jenny had said about Darla. Damn Crissman and Cheyenne Jones to hell for what they had caused the woman to do! She was in low spirits anyway over the death of Turner; it wouldn't have taken much to get her to talk — plenty of whiskey, perhaps, or maybe pure fear. Whatever, after realizing she had betrayed him, she had chosen suicide as the way to still her grief — and conscience. Garnett swore deeply. He hoped he'd have the chance someday to make both men pay for what they had done to her.

And Jenny — she had answered the questions he'd put to himself about their future. *Let me know where you'll be and I'll meet you there*, she'd written. No qualms, no holding back, no indecision — just say where. And he would, as soon as he could decide what his next move would be.

Pulling away from the hitching rack, Frank headed back for the Benbow ranch. He'd take the day and get things in shape as much as he could. Then when he saw John Crissman ride in, he'd be ready to move on. The first thing on the list was to recover the steers driven off by Digger and the men who had been with him. It was not the value of the stock involved; it simply had to be made clear to Pooler and his crowd that rustling Amanda Benbow's cattle would not be tolerated.

CHAPTER
TWENTY-FOUR

Frank avoided the road from town to Benbow's, not because he feared an ambush — most of Dave Pooler's bunch were in the Red Bull — but because it saved time to cut across the range. Not only was he aware of the press of time and the need to accomplish as much as possible before he was forced to ride on, but he was also concerned for Rudy Schreiber, and he hoped to find Doc Gittleman still there so that he might have a talk with him.

But the physician had already ridden off, heading not back to town, Cully Smith reported from his perch on the bunkhouse steps, but on up the road to pay a call on a Mrs. Cartwright, who was expecting a baby.

"Said Rudy'd be all right, 'cepting he'll have to stay there on his bunk for a couple or three days."

Garnett nodded in relief. "Good to know he wasn't bad hurt," he commented, and dismounted.

"Sure was . . . You see Pooler?"

Frank nodded. "Claims he don't know anything about the rustling — and Digger and Irv weren't around. Told Pooler it made no difference, that I wanted the steers back with the rest of the herd by sundown."

"I reckon that shook him up a mite —"

"Didn't seem to. Something's going on that I don't know about. Anyway, all I can do is sit tight until sundown. If they haven't driven the stock back by then, I'll go in and settle up."

Cully pulled off his battered hat and rubbed at the back of his sun-reddened neck. Small, thin, and leathery, the years showed heavily on his slight frame.

"Well, I reckon you know what you're doing, but taking on that whole bunch for a dozen stinking cows —"

"It's not the steers — it's that the Pooler bunch have got to learn they can't just come in and help themselves to Benbow stock every time they need a little cash. I let it go, they'll nickel and dime the place to death."

Cully nodded, drew a plug of tobacco from his shirt pocket and gnawed off a corner. "Yeh, can see what you mean. They got to be learned a lesson."

"One they won't forget," Garnett said quietly. "Cully, I've got some talking to do to you."

The old cowhand spat, considered Frank wonderingly. "That so?"

"I'm putting you in charge of the ranch. Until Ira gets back, you'll be the foreman."

Smith gave that several moment's thought. "You just up and pulling out?"

"Will have to. Could be tomorrow, or maybe the next day."

"Don't hardly seem right you doing that — just going off, leaving the place flat —"

170

"Not that I want to," Garnett said. "I've got no choice. A time back I killed a man — a sheriff. There's been a U.S. marshal hunting me ever since. I got word this morning that he'd learned I was here and is on his way. Means I've got to get across the border."

Cully again spat. "Sure mighty bad all the boys ain't here. Way they feel about you, I reckon they'd be real pleased to take care of that tin star for you."

Frank shook his head. "I appreciate that, but I won't have any of you getting yourselves crosswise with the law. That marshal — name's John Crissman — is in the right, far as he knows. I got framed by a deputy sheriff and the marshal took his word over mine. Hope to straighten it all out one day."

Cully shrugged. "Expect you know best —"

"I'll fix things up in town for you to buy what you'll be needing until Amanda Benbow gets here. I'll try to find you some more help, too."

"That's what we're needing. With you leaving and Rudy laid up, I just don't know —"

"Do what you can."

"Yeh, that's all a mule can do, I reckon. What's next?"

"I'll be waiting down in that swale with the rest of the herd for Pooler to bring back those steers. If he does, that'll settle it. If not, I'll go into town after him. I still don't swallow that tale he give me — that he didn't know anything about the rustling."

"Me neither," Cully said, rising. "Best I go spell off Ollie. That new fellow you hired is inside sleeping. Can rouse him if you're of a mind."

"Let him be," Garnett said, starting toward the nearest corral with his horse. "I'll stand watch here till it gets close to sundown, then I'll go set with the herd. No matter how it turns out, you're in charge. Be up to you to handle things."

"I'll sure enough try," Cully said, moving off. Reaching his horse, he looked back. "Luck — friend."

Frank Garnett smiled, nodded. "Obliged — and the same to you."

The steers were not returned. Garnett waited until there was only a small, glowing arc of sun showing above the low hills to the west, and then concluding that Pooler had ignored his demand, mounted the bay and rode into town.

Halting first at the end of the street, he studied Zeke Hammer's office for a full five minutes, making certain there was no one else there with the old marshal. When he was finally convinced that John Crissman had not yet arrived, Frank moved on and swung into the rack at the rear of the Red Bull and dismounted.

As he started for the saloon's entrance, the rattle of chains and the pound of hooves brought him to a halt. Turning, he saw the westbound stage wheel into the far end of the street and come to a stop at the depot. Immediately Dave Pooler, trailed by Dillon and three other members of his crowd, came through the Red Bull's doors and sauntered toward the coach.

It could mean only one thing; Amanda Benbow was aboard the stagecoach, and Pooler was there to greet her. Continuing along the side of the saloon, Garnett reached the walk and took up a stand a few strides from the depot. An elderly man appeared in the doorway of the stage, dismounted, and then a young woman stepped into view. She hesitated briefly, and upon seeing Pooler quickly stepped down.

Amanda Benbow had changed considerably since he'd last seen her, Frank realized. Now, a grown woman, she was somewhat heavily built, had a wealth of blond hair and a round, doll-like face. She had her father's clear blue eyes, but other than that he could see little resemblance.

When she touched the ground, she hurried to Pooler and threw her arms about him. Dave turned his head, cast a sardonic smile and a broad wink at Pete Dillon and the others with him, and took the girl into his own embrace. Anger and concern swept Garnett. This was the last thing in the world Hiram Benbow would want — his daughter and the man he feared and despised getting together.

"Amanda — Miss Benbow!" Frank called sharply, moving in closer. "Like to talk to you — alone."

The girl drew back from Pooler, and they both turned. Pete Dillon also came about, eyes narrowing.

"Who are you?" Amanda asked, frowning.

"Name's Garnett. I'm a friend of your pa's."

The girl nodded. "He mentioned you — you and your brother — and a time back in Missouri, on the farm, when you stayed with us."

Amanda had a stiff, superior way to her, and she spoke in a voice that revealed her city education.

173

"That is the favor I'm repaying. Had a letter from your pa sometime before he died. Asked me to come here, drive Pooler and his crowd off the place, and take over for you."

Amanda was silent for a moment or two, then said, "My father never mentioned anything like that to me. Why would he do it?"

"Because Pooler's a thief," Frank said calmly, alert for any move on the part of Dave or Pete Dillion. "He and his bunch were stealing the place blind and letting it go to ruin while your pa was sick and couldn't do anything about it."

The girl looked at Dave and back to Garnett, a mixture of shock and surprise on her features. "I don't believe you!" she declared suddenly. "Dave would never do anything like that — and anyway, why wouldn't my father have told me about it? I think you're saying this because you want the ranch for yourself."

Pooler slipped an arm around the girl's shoulders. The anger Frank's words had stirred within him had faded, and he was now smiling.

"Told you she was smart," he said, nodding to his friends. "Told you that Garnett wasn't going to fool her!" Glancing down at the girl, he added, "You got it figured out right."

"He come riding in one day and made me and the boys I had working for me move out. Was some of the old hands sided with him. I just set back and let it go, because I knew you'd be coming soon and we could get it all straightened out — and that's what I reckon we ought to do before we marry up."

Marry! The word hit Frank Garnett with the force of a blow. Evidently Amanda and Pooler had been corresponding right along, and Dave, making the most of their past acquaintance, had convinced her of his love and proposed marriage. Pooler's earlier remark that he wasn't about to foul his own nest now made sense. By catering to Amanda's girlish fancies and making her his wife under the pretense of love, Pooler would become owner of the ranch, after which he could ignore her and resume his old way of life, bleeding the H-Bar-B dry.

He could not let that happen, Garnett decided, the anger within him building steadily. If he was to keep the pledge he had made to Hiram Benbow, he could not allow Pooler to get away with it. Somehow he must convince Amanda that Dave was no good, that he was a common thief, a rustler, and wanted her only for the easy living marrying her would provide.

"I'm not asking you to believe me," Frank said, glancing up the street where a dozen or more persons had paused to look on. "Go talk to Pettigrew — he's standing there in front of the bank. Was a friend of your pa's. He'll give you the straight story on this."

The girl frowned and glanced at Pooler. Dave shook his head. "Ain't no need."

"You scared to let her talk to him?" Garnett pressed.

Pooler shrugged. "Hell no, I ain't! Mandy knows what's what, and Pettigrew ain't going to change her thinking."

"Then let her go talk to him — unless she's scared to," Frank continued.

Amanda flung a burning glance at him. "I'm not afraid — but no matter what he says, it won't make any difference! I love Dave, and I'm going to marry him!" she declared, and head high, shoulders stiff, stepped off the walk and hurried across the street toward the bank.

CHAPTER
TWENTY-FIVE

Frank Garnett watched until Amanda Benbow had reached the bank, joined Pettigrew, and gone inside. He turned then to Pooler, his hard face an expressionless mask.

"Few things I aim to settle with you," he said.

Pooler waved off the statement. "Ain't no use worrying about them steers Digger and the boys took. I'm running the ranch from now on — and I'll —"

"You'll string along with them, that's what you'll do," Garnett cut in. "Pooler, you're a liar, a thief, and a no-account, woman-chasing boozer — and I'm not about to let you marry the daughter of a man I'm indebted to and ruin her life."

Frank's voice was strong, carried an edge, and was audible to all who were nearby. Pooler's eyes flickered with anger, and then he shrugged.

"You ain't got nothing to say about it. Girl's going to marry me."

A taut smile pulled down the corners of Garnett's mouth. "Only after I'm dead."

"Won't be no problem," Dave said coolly. "I got boys who'll take you on the minute I say the word."

"Why call on them? You a lousy coward, along with the other names I called you?" Frank taunted.

Again Pooler's eyes sparkled. "No — but I ain't no damn fool, either. Anyway, that's what I got Dillon for — him and a couple others."

"You had Red Hadley packing iron for you, too, but he didn't turn out to be so good. Maybe you ought to try your own hand, prove you can back up some of the big talk you make."

"Nope, I leave that to Pete and the boys. They can take you easy."

"Then tell them to get at it," Garnett snapped, and as he saw Dillon make his move, he drew and fired.

One of the men on Pooler's left made a frantic grab for his weapon in that same instant. Frank snapped a hurried shot at him, and as he saw the man stagger and start to fall, he caught a glimpse of Pooler's arm sweeping down and his hand reaching for the pistol on his hip. Garnett's grim smile became a grimace of satisfaction. He triggered his gun again, driving his third bullet into Dave's chest. Pooler yelled, rocked to one side, and sank into the loose dust.

Motionless, still ready, Garnett considered the remaining men, standing frozen by the lifeless bodies of their three friends.

"Anytime," Frank murmured, aware now of the sound of footsteps hurrying down the street. It would be Marshal Hammer, he reckoned.

The men seemed not to have heard Frank's softly spoken invitation at first, and then realizing what he had said, all shrugged and moved their hands well away from their weapons.

"Dave!"

The word was a shrill cry of agony that split the tense hush. Garnett took a step back as Amanda Benbow rushed past him and threw herself upon Pooler's crumpled shape. From nearby he heard Zeke Hammer speak.

"Was watching. Garnett was in the right — that bunch was crowding him. But I told him once I wouldn't stand for no shootings here and —"

Frank raised his glance to the lawman as he reloaded the .45 and slid it back into the holster. "It's all right, Marshal. I'll be pulling out."

His voice broke off as he caught sight of a solitary rider on the road well to the north. It could be John Crissman, and it could be just some cowhand on his way to town. It didn't matter; Crissman was coming, and if he didn't arrive that day, he would the following — or the one after that.

Suddenly Amanda Benbow was on her feet, pounding at his face and chest with small, clenched fists. Tears were streaming down her cheeks, and rage and grief filled her eyes.

"You — you — murderer! You've killed Dave, but it won't get you my ranch — not ever!"

Frank caught the girl by the wrists and pulled down her arms. "You don't have anything I want," he said quietly. "I came here because I owed your pa. I reckon I've repaid him."

Releasing his grip on the girl, Garnett turned and crossed to his horse. Mounting, he started to double back to the street.

"Ira Flagg and the rest of the crew will be getting back from that cattle drive soon," he said, directing his words to Hammer and Ed Pettigrew, who had now joined the crowd. "Flagg will take over running the ranch for the lady when he gets here. I'll be obliged if you'll see that she's looked after till then."

Pettigrew said, "Of course . . . You pulling out right away?"

"Right away," Frank replied, and as an idea came to him, added, "Always wanted to have a look at Mexico."

Touching the brim of his hat with a forefinger, he cut the bay gelding about and struck out for the ranch at a fast lope. Once there, he'd pick up his gear and head out — not for Mexico, but north for McCurdy. With U.S. deputy marshal John Crissman scouring the area around Santee's Crossing for him, what better time to return to home and Jenny?

And that would be a good time to back Cheyenne Jones into a tight corner and make him admit before witnesses that he'd lied about the murder of Tom January. After that, he and Jenny could go their way in peace.

Frank Garnett grinned wryly at the thought, noting idly as he did three men driving a dozen or so steers onto Benbow range. Peace was something he could use a full measure of in the days to come.